# Light
## A Tale of the Magical Creatures of Zudukii

T.S. McNally

LIGHT: A TALE OF THE MAGICAL CREATURES OF ZUDUKII

Cover Illustration provided by Selkie used with permission.

Copy editing work provided by Mary Hope Shaw.

Special thanks goes to my parents for allowing me the freedom to explore new worlds, keeping me from wandering too far from the path I needed to travel.

Print ISBN: 978-0-9860956-0-3

Printed in the United States of America

# Table of Contents

# Chapter 1
# Night of Transitions

He felt the ground meet his side and a sharp pain bellowed up through his torso as he felt the blades of grass tickle his muzzle fur. He closed his eyes, but could still hear the vicious music of kicks connecting with their target and the reverberating jeers and taunts of the chorus.

"Stop this," his voice cracked, "This isn't necessary."

A laugh rose up amongst the group. "Of course it's necessary. It's necessary because you're a wimp." The dark grey form's sharp, white teeth glistened as he flashed a grin in the light of the nearby torches that could be found strewn about the quiet village. "Look at the 'great leader', all covered in dirt and mud." The footpaw of the creature above him pressed down on his muzzle and forced it to the ground. "Eat the grubs within the soil. If you want to learn to fight, you need more meat in your diet."

The victim on the ground opened his eyes to see only the darkness of the footpad on his snout. He growled, his reply ringing through the night air despite having his muzzle suppressed. "Your actions are just part of a meaningless show and I will not humor you by turning it into a fight. You want me to get angry, you want me to be just like you. You can beat me until I'm unconscious. I refuse to let you change me."

"Beat you 'til you're unconscious? Why… I wasn't planning on doing that, but I guess we can arrange that now that you've so nicely suggested it." The footpaw rose, letting the one on the ground look up at the group of attackers above him, the leader of them still grinning down upon him.

The beaten one was quite familiar with the bully's smug face. Fangstro led his group of lackeys around as if to compensate for not being old enough to command Emergant village upon his father's passing. Resentment turned the wolf bitter against the current leadership, so the canine tormented their son at every opportunity.

As the wolf made his motion to kick the fallen one once again, another voice cut through the air. "It's Bomeran, let's get out of here!" The others started to run off, leaving only a scampering noise behind them. The wolf let out a humph as he put down his foot onto the ground, deciding not to risk getting a last kick in before his departure.

"Daddy came to save his precious little wimp, but some day, daddy won't be around to protect you, and then what will you do?" he sneered a bit, "Our tribe will fall at your leadership, and I think our clansmen will plainly see that you do not deserve the honor which should have been mine by birth."

The grey wolf faded into the shadows of the night, avoiding the main path of the village and following his colleagues. Relief swept over the victim that the bullies had fled, but it gave way to embarrassment and disappointment in himself as he felt his father's eyes fall upon him.

He stood and brushed himself off, regaining his composure. Before him now stood the large figure of a rugged forest buck. The large rack upon his head was imposing, even for those that were not seen as his enemy. Scars from the stag's previous battles decorated his imperfect, ten-point set of antlers. The right side's beam came to an abrupt end just past the surroyal antler. The asymmetry certainly made the older buck stand out among his peers.

"Garoo." The buck's low and bellowing voice boomed a bit even when making as calm and simple a statement as saying his son's name. It drew attention and made its presence known even when it was not shouting. In the rare occasion the buck did raise his voice, it could feel as if the very lands were trembling.

Obviously, this was true in the figurative sense, as being the leader of a tribe made the weight of Bomeran's word heavy indeed. He was extremely well-respected, as he had been a warrior mage in many of the Tri-Societal War's major battles. He had seen conflicts that his son's generation could probably only see in the most vivid of their imaginations, or darkest of nightmares. The scar upon the Elder's antlers was the most visible representation of those times, though hidden under the layer of brown fur were other scars both physical and emotional.

The stories that the buck's voice could cause the planet to shift, though, were more than just figurative in meaning. His father was a Land mage and blessed by the Powers with abilities that could shape the lands of Zudukii. Garoo, like most of his generation, had not seen these powers used in combat aside from occasional sparring matches. In these peaceful times they lived as farmers and now used their powers to help cultivate the land for growing crops. Despite not having seen it before, Garoo had little doubt that being able to summon up earthquakes was well within his father's power.

"Father." Garoo's voice was softer than his father's, and he could not bring himself to look up into the buck's eyes. His fur was scuffled and messy from being shoved into the ground and beaten upon by Fangstro and his posse.

"Son, look up when speaking."

"Sorry, dad," the adolescent apologized as he straightened, though he still felt a bit slack on the inside. He knew what was going to come next: the lectures about standing up for himself.

"Listen son, I know you think I'm going to lecture you about what just happened, but I've been down that road before. Since tonight is the night before you become an adult, I think I need to get used to not lecturing you anymore." With a somber nod, he rested a hoof on his son's shoulder.

A bit of relief had taken hold in Garoo, maybe at last he understood: violence just wasn't his way. He never understood why, he could just never bring himself to harm others, even if they meant him harm. It was something that brought a bit of conflict between his father and himself growing up. Now that he was older and capable of making his own decisions, maybe his father would stop getting on his case or trying to pressure him into violent action.

As Bomeran dropped his hoof back down to his side, he smiled. For a moment he simply gazed at his child, the flesh and blood of the one he had loved and lost. It amazed him how much Garoo had grown over the years.

Garoo had some of his father's characteristics, and was obviously his blood. His son had gotten his coloring from him for the most part: a tan overcoat with a splash of white under his tail and some lighter spots scattered about his torso. His offspring also had his own set of antlers. They were merely a four point set, however, and appeared to have stopped growing. Traditionally this would have been a very disappointing turn out for a stag, but the fact his son had any antlers at all was a blessing to Bomeran, and a pleasant surprise.

This was because his child was not a pure-blooded stag.

His son took mostly the form of his mother. Garoo's tail was large and long, with a thick base which tapered down to a tip. His tail's strength put his father's own tail to shame. His ears were longer, standing tall over his four-point antlers. Unlike his father's hooves, Garoo's footpaws were long and clawed.

"It's odd in a way, despite the fact that I have raised you, you still have your mother's spirit. She, too, was stubbornly peaceful in her ways. I know she would be proud of you, and the fact that tomorrow you'll begin your journey into adulthood." He leaned in a bit and spoke softly the next part: "And if it's any consolation, I do believe Fangstro's father would not have put up with his behavior, nor would he have been proud of it. It is truly a shame."

The kangaroo gave a nod, smiling a bit to his father. "Thanks dad, that means a lot to me." He glanced back at the party taking place in the village square, where he had just come from. The wolf and his gang had moved on to ravaging the food banquet around the large bonfire.

"As I said, I don't want to hold you with any lectures. Tonight is a time of celebration; you and your friends have a lot of work to do tomorrow. However, I would like you to stop by my hut before heading back to our home."

When his father referred to his hut, Garoo looked a bit confused. Usually talking with Bomeran in the tribal Elder's meeting hut was a large deal reserved for important matters of business. He had never spoken with his father there, only in the more casual environments such as the village commons or their own home.

"Sure dad, I'll be there in about an hour. I'm not really in the mood for celebrating all that much."

His father shook his head. "Son, trust me, enjoy the good times while they are here, for tomorrow you may be wishing for today." He then turned to leave, moving in the direction of the chieftain's hut. "We have a lot to discuss before your journey tomorrow, clear your head and enjoy the night."

With his father's egress, the kangaroo looked back toward the party. Villagers were dancing around a large fire in the center, having a rowdy time of it. Fathers and mothers looked on, proud of this new stage for the next generation. Tomorrow they'd be heading to the Omnigic village found in the jagged valleys to the north of their shoreside village. There the adolescents would ascend into adulthood and become magic users themselves — or at least those worthy would. Sometimes the Powers didn't look with favor upon a few souls and left them as powerless as when they began their journey. Typically, the tribes shunned the powerless, placing them on the lowest tier of society. It was harsh, but it was tradition. It made the whole situation all the more nerve-wracking for all involved.

The roo had moved toward the party as he thought about the day ahead. He smiled to himself when he spotted a large bear scarfing up large quantities of food. Just who he was looking for.

"Hey, Urand," Garoo called in greeting. The bear, however, did not reply, as the sounds of unmannered eating and the bowl before the creature's face obscured any sound of Garoo's words.

"Urand!" he shouted, causing the bear to choke a bit as he put the plate down.

With a cough and a few thumps to his chest, Urand's eyes watered as he finally responded. "Oh, hey there, runt." The name was not quite an insult, as he called pretty much anyone smaller than him runt, which actually accounted for most of the tribe. Despite being the same age, Urand was a bear in true name and form. "Want some grub? You best get some, I'll have it gone within the hour."

Garoo shook his head a bit. "Just thinking about tomorrow. My father wants me to come to the hut tonight and talk over something."

The bear cocked his head. "Really? He requested my sister do the same."

"Kareen?" Urand's sister and Garoo were very good friends. Typically there were no secrets between them. Why then, Garoo wondered, had this been kept from him?

The bear suddenly choked on his food again, his eyes widened. "Oh! I wasn' supposed to tell you about that. Don't tell my sis' I told you! She will be furious!"

"Why? What's the big deal?" Garoo asked.

"She just wanted to surprise you is all. I am so bad at keeping secrets. Why did you tell me sis? Why? Why?"

He was definitely panicking. "Please don't tell her! Act surprised when you see her there."

"You know my acting isn't my best talent, and neither is lying," the roo shook his head. "Really, I don't see what the big deal is, in fact I was just going to talk to her about it. Where is she, anyway? I haven't seen her around the party."

"You promise you won't tell her?"

"I can promise I won't tell her, but you know her; she'll know that I know without me saying anything."

The bear sighed. "You're right about that—can't hide anything from sis." He gestured into the darkness toward the docks and the kangaroo instantly knew that she was probably swimming. In fact, as an otter, Kareen was pretty much in the water almost every time he saw her. Even with this party going on she was off swimming at night. "Just don't let father find out she's down there. He doesn't like it when she swims in the dark."

Garoo smiled a bit. "I never have. I don't think she's one bit afraid of him though, so I don't think she cares if he knows or not."

"Yeah, sis is crazy like that." Urand agreed.

Garoo gave a nod to the bear. "Can't argue that. Enjoy the meal, but don't eat too much—I don't want to have to roll you up onto the barge tomorrow."

"Hmph. Make fun of my eating habits again and I'll roll you off the boat, runt." He gave a grunt and then a laugh, steadfastly ignoring Garoo's dietary advice as his friend headed for the shoreline.

Crisp scent came up from the shore as the sound of soft waves filled the large ears of the kangaroo. The deep orange moon up in the sky reflected off the waters of the coast. It was full on this night and the tide was high. He knew he was getting close when he heard a splash coming from beyond the far dock.

He spied her as she seemed to glide through the water, her back barely visible, but he had gotten used to seeing it within the surface of the bay. He sat down and watched her quietly, not wanting to interrupt the creature as she made her way serenely. Garoo smiled a bit as he watched her, she always seemed most at peace here, moving along the waves, at one with the water. Her paws barely grazed along the surface as her body slid along, causing the moon's reflection to quiver and dance in her wake.

Garoo made his way out to the edge of the dock. He moved quietly as to not disturb her from her time with the bay. He always did enjoy watching her swim, though he didn't much care for the water himself.

Sitting down, he got a better view of her sliding along the surface, the otter unaware of his presence as she mingled in her natural environment. The moment was quiet; all was calm.

"Whatcha doin'?"

"Gah!" Garoo was startled. The quiet moment shattered as his feet splashed against the surface of the water. He looked over his shoulder to find a fawn with a sly grin on his face as if he'd known he was interrupting something important. "Lyle! What are you doing out so late?" Garoo snapped impatiently.

"Seein' what brudder doin'," Lyle responded to his older half-sibling. Garoo sighed a bit, having brothers could be a pain, and if a half brother was this bothersome he could only imagine how much trouble a full one could be. Since Garoo's mother had died right after his birth, the blood shared between him and the little deer present was only that of their father.

"You should be in bed back home," Garoo lectured.

"Is brudder hanging out wif his ladyfriend?" the little one teased.

"Would you be quiet? She doesn't even know that I'm here!" he gestured impatiently in attempts to shoo away the youngster. "If you leave now I won't tell dad you were out this late, and I'll even sneak you a toffee from the party."

"Toffee!" he smiled. "Okay brudder, jus' no K-I—uh—C-C-I—and-G."

"Kiccig?" the older one teased. "I certainly won't be doing any of that."

"Kissing!" he whined. "You knew what I meant, brudder."

"Aren't you a bit young to be talking to your brother about kissing?" a voice called. Garoo's head whipped around to see the head of the otter peering out from the dimly-lit waters. It appeared the kangaroo's cover was blown.

"Nuh uh, I'm old 'nough." Lyle stuck his tongue out at her. She retaliated by splashing the fawn with water. "Hey!" The youngster cried out at the shock of suddenly being wet. "Why you splash me? He was da one spying on you!"

The kangaroo flushed as he turned to his brother to shout. "I was not spying, you liar!" he then goes silent for a bit. It wasn't like him to shout, he was just worried she might take offense to the prospect of being spied on. "Listen, if you aren't gone in five seconds, I won't get you a toffee from the party."

The young buck sasses his older brother. "You just wanna play kisshy face is all."

"One—" Garoo started to count as he went to stand up.

10

"Alright… Alright. Sheesh, I'm goin'. You better bring me back a toffee d'ough!" With that, the fawn turned and made his way from the shore. Garoo let out a sigh of relief. Now that his brother was gone, he could get back to peace and quiet and talk with Kareen about the current matter.

"Brothers are a pain." The kangaroo shook his head a bit.

"He'll grow out of it in time, you'll see," the otter replied as she leaned onto the dock. She peered over to Garoo standing on the wooden planks before her and smiled up to him lightly. "Anyway, were you spying on me?" she asked.

The roo turned around and shook his head. "W-What of course not."

She lifted herself out of the water, her slick fur shining in the moonlight. With a playful grin Kareen lightly flicked the roo's nose. "You've always been a terrible liar." She shook her head. "So why are you not at the party?"

"I was going to ask you the same thing," the roo countered.

The otter crossed her arms over chest a bit. "Well, I asked first so it's only fair that you answer first."

"Hmph. Aren't you cold? You should dry off or something."

Kareen gave the difficult roo's shoulder a punch. "Don't change the subject on me, you know that I am quite more comfortable being wet then I am dry. I am a water mage through and through."

The kangaroo shook his head. "Well, you seem confident, that's not really up for you to decide what you will become." However, she did spend so much time in the water, if she were to be anything else it would truly be a tragedy. Water mages took up many jobs including the fishing, irrigation, and some could even make it rain if drought took hold. To be able to swim as well as she and not behold the life around the water would certainly be unfortunate. Yet still, one's job was not decided upon by the individual, but during their journey to the Omnigic Temple and only the Powers would decide the fate of each.

She gave a laugh. "I'd better be. Haven't you ever dreamt of which element you'd be gifted with?"

Garoo was thrown off by that question. "I... haven't really thought about it. I guess I'd want to be a land mage like my father."

She thinks. "Well, you seem rather well grounded, but I don't think you are really built that way."

"What's that supposed to mean?" He asked, slightly offended.

"Well, you don't really stand your ground. You're not all that firm."

Garoo stuck his tongue out. "You sound like my dad. You think I'm going to be a mage of the winds?"

She smiled at the thought. Usually they worked paw-in-paw with those of the water affinity, as generating rain is difficult without airflow and currents. They could also help sail-powered ships move more quickly though the waters.

"That would be interesting wouldn't it? I don't think there's been a wingless mage of wind in a long time, though." She then frowned a bit. "Hey! You didn't answer my question."

The kangaroo grinned. "What question was that?" A quick jab to his arm caused the roo to yelp in pain.

As Garoo shook a bit from the punch, she realized that the cry was not entirely playful. At first she worried that she had hit him too hard, but upon further investigation she could see bruising along his arms. With that information it was clear why he had left the party. "I see. Was it Fangstro?" The otter asked softly.

"He wasn't the reason I left, no," the horned roo replied with a shake of his head. "I would have went back, but, I wanted to tell you about the meeting we were going to."

As soon as he said those words he wanted to take them back; it was probably somewhere between his brother and the jolt of pain, but he just then remembered that he wasn't supposed to know that she was going with him.

"We? How did you know about that?" Kareen pondered for a short period but then sighed as she realized the answer. "My brother can't keep a secret to save his life. I guess I have no one to blame but myself for the fact I told him. I was pretty excited though, it's not often that people are invited into that hut, and it's always for important things. I wonder what he wants to talk to us about."

"For you to stop hitting me, maybe," said Garoo with a chuckle.

"Hitting you?" She gave a softer punch to his side as to not agitate the bruising. "If it were about that I'm sure Fangstro would have had a front row seat."

"True, but I guess we should head up to find out, and to do that, like it or not, you're going to have to dry off."

"Yeah and so do you…" she retorted.

He looked to her, confused. "I am dry already."

A moment too late he realized her intent. A few seconds and a loud splash later, Garoo found himself in the water while a laughing otter stood on the dock

"Well," she breathed between giggles, "you were!"

The kangaroo lifted his torso up so that his upper body leaned up over the dock. His fur was sopping wet. He took a moment to shoot a glare up at her. "Very funny."

The otter shook her head, still smirking to herself as she offered out her paw to help him. Garoo reached up and gripped as if to accept the helping paw, only to grin mischievously and pull.

About an hour had passed when the tribal leader had two damp adolescents at his door. He shook his head a bit and simply stated. "You're late."

"Sorry dad. Bit of a situation at the docks," the kangaroo replied.

The elder deer looked to the two, as their fur was still damp from their swim. His son's fur was a bit disheveled, as he wasn't really built for looking that elegant after being in the water. The otter wore it much better. She smiled a bit. "We took care of it though, not really an emergency. So, why did you want to see us?"

Bomeran gave a nod to the two as he let them into the central meeting hut. Garoo had seen it from time to time, never on official business of course, as children were usually not a part of the affairs of adults and village matters until after they had journeyed through the Transition. It felt taboo for them to be there, which only made him more anxious to know exactly why they'd been invited in the first place.

"I'm glad you took my advice to enjoy yourself Garoo," his father stated as he sat down. "This is a good time to spend with friends, as when you grow up, the Powers may lead you down separate roads that may cause you to see less of one another." There was a moment of somber silence as the older deer took a deep breath. "Come sit down."

Both the kangaroo and otter moved to the sides of central circle to settle into their own low chairs. Garoo for the life of him could never get his thick legs to cross in such a way as other animals could. It was a combination of his larger feet and thigh structure. Instead he sat upon his lower legs in a kneeling-down position. Kareen was just fine and comfortable taking a similar seating posture as Bomeran who sat cross-legged.

As soon as the adolescents were ready, he looked among the two. "You two have a big day ahead of you tomorrow, so I shall be as brief as possible." The large buck reached over and put a hoof to his son's shoulder, speaking only after he released a quiet sigh. "Son, the reason I have brought you and your friend here is that I have come to a decision lately. This was not easy for me, and it took a lot of time and reconciliation, but through all my contemplations I feel it is the best course of action for the village. The village is far more important than the difficulty the decision brings on me, and the strain I feel to announce this to you."

Garoo closed his eyes, he'd had a feeling this day would come. While the foreboding talk would not come as a surprise to the young roo, he knew how hard it must be for his father to go through with it.

"It's about me, isn't it?"

Bomeran nodded, a rare look of difficulty in his eyes as he spoke. "Judging by your past behavior, and how you handle confrontation… I'm at an impasse. I am leaning towards having the responsibility of chief being passed on to another as opposed to passing it onto you."

Though Garoo had known this was coming, somewhere deep down it was still a jolt. It felt a strange mix of being accepted and rejected at the same moment.

A moment of heavy silence fell over the hut. The father waited quietly to see his son's reaction once he had a chance to absorb the news. However, the first to stir the pot was none other than the female otter.

"With all due respect, why was I required to be here for this?" she asked looking from Garoo to the Elder. "Surely you could have told him without me here."

Bomeran gave a bit of a nod. "Well, this decision will affect you as well Kareen, for if I do decide to remove my son from the position I feel you would make a fine replacement."

Kareen looked surprised, and at the same time upset. "You're asking me to take this position from my friend? What about his brother? Surely if the position is supposed to stay in family lines he would take it! I don't want to steal your family's birthright! Are you just going to let him do this Garoo?" she looked over to the roo with a bit of a glare. "This is your position, don't let him just give it away like this!"

Garoo sighed, shaking his head as he crossed his arms in front of his chest. "It's his to give. If he feels I don't deserve it then that is his decision. And quite frankly, I'm glad he chose you as the replacement rather than some of the others who could have been viable candidates in this tribe," he said, his mind immediately going to the wolf who had pounded him into the ground earlier.

The Elder stag nodded in agreement and looked back to Kareen. "This conversation is the very reason I think you'd make the best candidate. You do believe in fighting when your back is to the wall; when your future or those of your friends looks dire."

Garoo frowned. "Why is fighting necessary? You tell me all the time of the Powers and how they guide us through life. If everything is decided, then why is fighting to change it necessary? Do we feel ourselves better than them? If leading means that I'll be the one deciding people's fates in the Powers' stead, I think I'd prefer not to."

Bomeran gave him a curious glance. "Well, I haven't decided to go through with relinquishing your position quite yet. I was simply giving you a warning. I wish to wait and see what the Higher Powers have to say on the matter. You will both be going through the trials at the Omnigic Temple, and will earn the abilities of our race. I will base my final decision off of the results of the ritual." He glanced between the two. "Clearly whoever the powers decide to be the more powerful mage amongst you will truly be ready to lead."

"Why not just give it to her? I just told you I really don't want to be in charge over others."

With a bit of a sigh, the stag looked back to his son. "Now who is the one making decisions in the Powers' stead? You have the peaceful stubbornness of your mother. And while I never fully understood it, I believe it could be of merit. Kareen, otherwise has the philosophy that I personally feel would make a great leader. Both of you I understand don't want the position, but when I first had it given to me I did not either."

"Then why did you take it?" the otter asked.

"Because those were the cards the Powers gave me. Though you may both not wish to be leaders, I think what you'll come to understand is that the best of leaders are not the ones who want to lead, but those who are reluctant and forced to do so."

The night had gotten just a bit darker as the two left the building behind them. The smell of smoke from the bonfire carried all the way down the path to their noses. They followed the trail back toward the other tribe members, watching the bodies grow larger as they approached from a distance.

"I still don't see why he couldn't just give it to your brother." Kareen broke the silence with a sigh. "I don't think it's fair to either of us to be told we're competing over our futures. He shouldn't expect friends to do that."

The male antlered kangaroo shook his head. "You're only allowed to pass the position to your first born. Otherwise, according to the tradition, you have to go outside the family. Not many know that."

"The traditions are strange sometimes—I mean some things I can understand, but something like that? It's his position, why not give it to whoever he wants?" She raised her questioning voice as not to be drowned by the noise of the party.

Garoo started to pick at the buffet. "Your brother has almost picked this clean," he joked. "He is giving it to who he wants, he just sees more of him in you, I suppose. What I don't understand is why he was with my mother, if he didn't see her qualities as good. He keeps saying that I have her qualities, as if it were a bad thing." He remembered to pick up some toffees for his brother.

In the silence that followed he looked to her and noticed her lack of interest in the buffet. "Aren't you hungry?"

She smiled wanly, clearly worried that she might end up taking the position she really felt belonged to her friend. Reluctantly the otter picked up a plate and started to put items on it. "You're not upset at all about this?" she asked.

"I am a little upset that he feels me incompetent, but as far as leading goes? I'm not going to be upset if I don't have to. I'm more worried if the worst happens tomorrow, if the so-called 'Powers' see me as unworthy as he does."

The otter hushed him and looked about, before leading them over to a more secluded area where they could continue the conversation. They found a pair of stumps away from the buffet and sat down with their plates in paw. "Don't say that! You could get in trouble if you question them too loudly, and I don't want to see you banished. I know you've always had your doubts in those old tales, but if our people have survived through a war standing by them, I think they've done our kind more good than harm."

In reply, the kangaroo shook his head. "How do we know those tales didn't start the wars? Think about it: if talking ill of the Powers is enough to be punished here, what would we do to outsiders that didn't believe? We've heard the stories of the Tri-Societal War, but it's all from our perspective. What of the other two societies? How did they view it? And why don't we know why it ended? Who won?"

Kareen shook her head in exasperation. "You ask too many questions, sometimes things just are."

A voice cut through the conversation, the timbre sending a chill up Garoo's spine.

"I knew you would make a terrible leader, but a blasphemer of the Powers? You really are pathetic." Fangstro was suddenly there, grinning ferally as he stared down at them through piercing eyes.

"Leave us be, wolf," Kareen warned as she turned to him.

Fangstro gave a dry laugh, his teeth glinting in the firelight. For once he was alone; normally he picked fights while accompanied by his younger sister and their posse.

"You going to let your girlfriend do your fighting for you again?" he jeered at Garoo.

"She's not my—"

"—Well at least you had the guts to come and cause trouble without your sister this time," The female otter huffed back, cutting off Garoo's indignant response.

"She's tougher than your boy, here," he grunted. "Of course that isn't saying much, a summer breeze could probably blow him over."

The kangaroo sighed. "Kareen, can you please just ignore him? He's just looking to fight. I don't want to give him what he's looking for."

With a laugh, the otter smiled. "Some individuals should be aware of what they seek, for they may not like what they get once they find it."

Fangstro shook his head. "Oh, don't make me laugh; he's not a fighter. As I've heard his father say, he's just like his mother. And what happened to his mother? She rolled over and died. So I think when it comes to an actual fight, if I were looking for one I'd search elsewhere."

Garoo glared at him; the comment had stung. His paw balled up to a fist, almost allowing himself to give in and wallop him across his snout. After a bit, though, he took a deep breath and relaxed, he knew this was just another ploy to goad him to react.

The otter was not going to let the words go unreturned, though, "Oh? Well if survival of one's parents is the measure of one's ability to handle oneself in a fight, then you'd probably wind up just like your father did."

The wolf snapped his attention away from the roo. His voice sounded choked, as though she hit him straight in the gut. "What… did you just say?"

"You heard me," Kareen replied.

"My father died with honor! He died fighting for our culture! For our kind! How dare you!" Without another word, the wolf had lunged at her. She had expected this; Fangstro was known for his hot temper. As the wolf's paw came in to collide with the otter's face, she moved her head to the side, causing the punch to miss. Without waiting for him to withdraw, her paws reached up and grabbed the now outstretched arm. She then shifted her weight backwards, pulling at the arm. Her feet came up and pushed into the canine's torso as she rolled backwards, sending him sailing over her to land on his back with a thud.

Before he had a chance to get his bearings she hopped up and straddled over him pinning him to the ground. "Not so tough without your posse, are you?"

Garoo frowned to himself. With barely a breath, he stood up and started back to his family's hut. He had grown weary of all the scuffles that day. She clearly seemed to have the situation under control, and he really didn't want to get involved.

Unaware that her friend had left, the otter remained astride Fangstro, a cocky grin upon her face. The dark grey canine snarled, "If you don't get off this moment, I'll—"

"You'll what?" she retorted. "Cry for your sister to help?" She glanced up briefly towards where Garoo was sitting earlier, about to ask him how she should deal with the beast, when she realized that his seat now lay empty. The otter leaned up to scout around, trying to find out where her companion had gone off to. As she searched, her weight lifted off the wolf below.

"Garoo? Where did you go?" she called out, barely able to finish her sentence when the wolf snarled and took advantage of the situation. Shifting himself around so that now he was pinning her to the ground, his clawed paws raised up in a threatening manner.

"You insolent wench! How dare you!" he bellowed with rage as his paw came down to strike her.

However, while the wolf concentrated his power into the blow, the otter found herself relatively unrestrained. Before the wolf's paw could reach her face, she was able to move her head out of the way and counter with her own blow, which connected across Fangstro's snout. She then used her thick tail to help leverage herself up, knocking off her reeling opponent. The stunned wolf fell off and onto the dirt on his back as the otter stood up.

Kareen brushed herself off and cleared her throat. Her eyes glancing about and looking for her friend, but he was nowhere to be found. His food was nearby and relatively untouched, also it appeared that he had left behind the toffees meant for his brother. She sighed as she picked them up.

"Garoo?" she called out again as she started to move away, no longer concerned about the wolf. A fresh stream of blood flowed down his nose and dripped off his dark furred muzzle.

As she had moved off into the distance heading toward Garoo's hut, a crowd started to gather around the scene, including Fangstro's sister. She moved to her brother's side, oblivious to what had happened as she helped him up. "Are you okay, brother?"

Fangstro's paw reached to stem the flow of blood from his nose. Below his breath, and barely audible to even his sibling, the canine growled.

"She will pay for this…"

"Garoo!"

The kangaroo let out an audible sigh. He withdrew his paw from the door he was about to open and turned around to see an upset otter.

"Why did you leave me back there?!" Kareen shouted at him, "I could have needed your help!"

The kangaroo let out another tired sigh. With such a big day ahead in the morning he really wanted to be well rested, but it now seemed as if it would have to wait.

"We both know you can handle yourself. You don't need my help when it comes to fighting. I'm tired; besides, you're the one who egged him on, so you could deal with the outcome on your own."

"I egged HIM on?" she frowned, "He was insulting your mother! The woman who gave birth to you! You were just going to let him do that?"

The kangaroo turned back to the door and opened it, shaking his head. "Nothing that wolf could say could ever change who my mother was, her life spoke for itself. His words hold little value when it's clear his motive was to stir me into hostility."

She grasped at her ears in frustration. "Argh! I'm not gullible! You may think I am, Garoo, but what he was trying to accomplish was not to simply demean your mother. It was to discredit you. When someone tries to do that, you have to stand up for yourself."

Garoo stepped into his home, pausing to gaze out at her. She seemed to be teary-eyed.

"I did stand up for myself, Kareen. Had I attacked him over meaningless words, then he would have won, for I would have lost myself. Good night, I'll see you in the morning, alright?"

Not waiting for her to answer, he shut the door. For a moment he simply stood and stared at the floor and the patches of moonlight which streamed across the room. But when he turned his gaze up to head for his room, he nearly jumped to the ceiling.

"Brudder! You have my toffee?" his young brother inquired as he leaned forward.

"By the Powers! You trying to give me a heart attack Lyle?!" he placed a paw on his chest. "Well, you see... I kind of..." He sighed as he felt his head start to ache. In all the excitement he knew he had forgotten something. He started to speak when there was a knock on the door. "Hold on a second." Garoo sighed as he turned back to open the door.

"We'll talk in the mor-" he was cut off as a satchel hit him in the nose, the cloth bag caught his upper snout and hung off of it like a coat hanger. The smell of toffee suddenly filled his nose.

"You forgot these." the otter stated before moving away from the door back into the darkness of the night.

After a stunned moment, he pulled the sack from his face and peered within to look upon the treats. "Thanks." he said to the night air as he turned around and shut the door behind him.

# Chapter 2
# Journey of the Arcane

Creatures of the night seemed more verbose than Garoo had recalled them being on evenings prior. Every time he went to close his eyes, the repetitive hooting and screeching jarred him from any solace of slumber. Though, perhaps his mind was just deflecting blame. The true bugs that kept him from being at ease were not those outside, but those causing his stomach to churn.

As much as he had played that he was ready to accept whatever fate decided to throw at him in the coming days, he was only mortal and was certainly not immune to the pressure bestowed upon him. His future and the future of those he cared for would be heavily affected by the upcoming turn of events.

Many in his culture typically turned to prayer in cases like these to ask the Powers for guidance or assistance in the tasks ahead. Garoo, however, wasn't one for doing such things. It wasn't that he was absolutely sure they did not exist, but he felt that if powerful and omnipresent beings existed it would be insulting to tell them what needed to be done. What business did any mortal such as he have in trying to dictate the actions of those better fit to make decisions about the course of events?

To ask beings such as them to help him would certainly be an insulting underestimation of them. Even worse, he would be personifying himself as some kind of essential messenger, when really he was but a kangaroo among the millions of creatures with which he shared the planet.

He sat at the window and looked up into the night sky, curious as to what time it was. It felt as if he had been up an eternity. He wondered what Kareen was up to and if she were having the same problems with trying to get some sleep.

Urand threw a pillow at his sister's bed from across the room. "Sis, you're snoring again!" the bear whined as he sat up in his bed.

While the projectile had landed on target, it had little effect on the loud, continuous rumbling. The bear sighed; now he had thrown away the only instrument he could use to cover his ears and muffle the racket. He wondered how he was ever going to get to sleep.

The problem might not have been the snoring, however. His stomach felt a bit off. Whether this was caused by the food or the big day ahead he could not determine, but the snores certainly weren't helping.

As the loud sound of the otter's reverberating throat continued, the bear finally abandoned his bedding and rolled off the side to the floor with a grumble. He crawled over to the side of the noisy sleeper's bed, his ears peering over the side like that of a shark's fin sneaking up on its prey.

"Sis!" the bear whispered harshly. He didn't want to risk disturbing the other occupants of the dwelling, so he kept his voice down. All Urand received in response was another snort from the otter, seemingly a bit louder in tone than the ones prior.

Now a bit annoyed, the otter's brother decided that he was going to risk waking her up just for some peace and quiet, in a relative sense of the term. He placed his paw on his sister's shoulder and started to shake. With a groan, she started to rouse from slumber and grumbled. She grabbed her pillow and started to wail on her brother with the soft mallet.

"Ow! Stop! Sis! It's me!" Urand whined as he put his paws over his head to defend against the blows.

The pillow stopped its assault upon the bear as Kareen sat up to see her brother. "Urand!" she let out a yawn. "I was sleeping! You'd better have a good reason for waking me up."

"Well... I can't sleep with you snorin' like that, sis."

There was a bit of a pause before the otter frowned and then took the pillow in her paw and threw it at her brother. "Snoring means that I'm asleep, you dolt! That's not a good reason to wake me!"

She stretched out and looked over to the bear with weary eyes as he sat upon the floor. "I've seen you sleep through much more obnoxious noises than a simple snore, is there something else bothering you?"

Urand let out a bit of a sigh. "How are you able to sleep, sis? I mean, so much is going to happen tomorrow. The rest of our lives could be laid out by what happens. How can you not be nervous?"

With the question she slid her legs to the side and sat on the edge of the bed. After letting out another yawn she gave an answer. "Of course I am a bit nervous, but, at the same time I know that whatever the outcome that my life isn't going to be everything I hoped for. Either I'm going to be stuck in this small town, or Garoo will be, either way it would be a little disappointing."

Her brother appeared a bit confused. "And how do you know those are the outcomes?"

She hesitated to answer, "I don't know if I'm allowed to tell. I mean, if I tell you I know I might as well tell everyone."

The bear frowned. "Are you still upset about me telling Garoo about that meeting? He would have found out soon enough."

She laughed. "Not the point. However, I wasn't told to keep this a secret, so I guess it wouldn't hurt to let you in on it. At the meeting I was told that I might become the next Elder of Emergant instead of Garoo."

"Really? Wow! That's amazing sis!" He cringed, realizing he'd said that a bit too loud. Immediately he softened his voice, mindful of the sleeping occupants of the house. "I mean… how's Garoo taking it?"

"He's okay with it. Though, Bomeran says that whoever the Powers decide is the better of us, they will get the responsibility. So either way, that means either him or I will be staying here. I was kind of hoping to get out there on the ocean, to see what's out there…"

Her words began to drift off on her hopes and dreams, a story her brother had heard many times before. Being a member of a shipping vessel to start, maybe getting enough recognition to have her own ship, then maybe someday a larger vessel to explore every corner of the large blue bodies of water that covered Zudukii.

"… but, a part of me was hoping that Garoo would be able to come with me. Now, no matter the outcome, it doesn't look like there will be any possibility of that happening." She finally stopped her monologue, realizing how she had carried on.

"Brother?" she asked as she noted he was being very quiet suddenly. Urand was now dead asleep on the floor, and, as if in response to the question, let out a loud guttural snore. Kareen let out a bit of a frustrated sigh. How was she going to sleep with all that racket?

The morning eye glowed red on the day of departure and peered over the horizon of the bay. The eyes of the creatures congregating upon the docks shared this quality with the sky, as the excitement of the night had kept them from slumber. Continuing to stream down the land towards the water's edge, a river of individuals flooded over the sturdy docks as they awaited the arrival of the ship that would take them, or their family members, to their destination of adulthood.

Garoo was sitting upon the edge of the pier, as he was one of the first to arrive long before the fiery glow of the new day joined the company. The crowd had grown to such a size that the kangaroo wrapped his tail around one of the posts as to keep himself from accidentally falling into the water. Not that hanging around Kareen didn't get him used to being wet, it was just a little too cool to have sopping wet, dripping fur. Swimming would also not be the best idea in a space where a ship would be docked momentarily.

The smells of the morning air were filled with cooked meats typically eaten around this time of the day. It was as if last night's party had migrated to probably the most inconvenient of areas. Maneuvering around the pier would be too difficult and was hardly worth the effort to get to the food in Garoo's mind, though his stomach started to remind him that he hadn't had much to eat this morning or the night prior. Being reminded of leaving behind that plate the previous evening made the kangaroo think about Kareen, and if she were still mad at him. Well, she probably still was, or at least would pretend to be anyway, knowing her stubbornness.

While the creatures around him spoke louder and louder as their numbers increased, Garoo was beginning to remember why he normally liked living here. Large crowds like this didn't settle too well with him. This town was normally a quiet one. It certainly wasn't like living in one of the four elemental capitals. Most of those in the crowd hailed from the capital of the land province, Floreinna, which was pretty much a landlocked city found deep in the forests about two days travel to the east. So in order for those coming of age to participate, those from the capital traveled here to hitch a ride on the large ship that traveled up north to the Omnigic Temple.

The crowd started to stir at that point in his musings, which caused the kangaroo to look up and to tighten his tail around the post at the dock's edge. Creatures peered over each other at the horizon as the tops of sails appeared from a few miles out. It was a special vessel that was only used for this journey, a large wooden ship that normally harbored in the water capital, on an island very far off. Every settlement of their race celebrated the Night of Transitions on a different evening depending on the amount of time it'd take to make their journey to the temple

"The Arcane is really a sight, isn't she?" a voice asked from out of nowhere. Garoo turned and looked over his shoulder. His father suddenly was standing pretty much right behind him, making him wonder if sneaking up behind people was a family trait.

He gave a bit of a nod. "Every time I've seen her come by, I've always been amazed that something that large can float," he said. Luckily, the dock was big enough to handle her, if just barely.

"This time is a bit different though." He smiled as he placed a hoofed paw upon the roo's furred shoulder. "You get to go aboard and see it from the inside, there's a lot to learn on the way there, but I don't think it'll be anything you can't handle. You were always pretty bright."

The crowd started to shift a bit, causing the father and son to turn their heads back inland. The sea of bodies on the dock seemed to part ways for a creature as it made its way toward the front of the dock where Bomeran and Garoo stood. Enveloped in a long green dress, a grey bushy form of a squirrel female started to make her way toward them. She had a litter of younglings in tow, some quite literally, clinging to her thick grey tail and playing about in the tufts. Oddly it seemed she didn't pay them any mind even though her children's behavior starkly contrasted her professional demeanor. She looked up and smiled in a way one would to an old friend. "Oh, Bomeran, glad to find you here."

"Ah, Lady Wollnutt, this is a pleasant surprise. I believe you have met my son, Garoo? He's going to be going to the Omnigic Temple this time. I came to see him off," Bomeran stated.

She turned to face the kangaroo, "Oh my! How the fires in the sky move so quickly! He certainly has grown a bit since I had last seen him, I wonder if you even remember who I am."

Garoo thought hard for a moment, feeling awkward. "Well... I don't remember the honor of meeting you my Lady, but of course I know who you are: you're the Sage of Land." In their culture everyone knew of the four elemental Sages, gifted individuals whose headquarters rested within the Omnigic Temple. They were in charge of each of their own Provinces, one for each element. Elders, like Bomeran, were only in charge of their own town, merely a subset of each Province.

The squirrel gave a smile which showed off her larger front incisors as she gave a nod. "Oh, I wouldn't expect you to remember our meeting, my dear roo." Garoo pondered the ambiguity of whether she said "dear roo" or "deer-roo" but shook it off as, in the end, it didn't quite matter.

Bomeran gave a nod, "You must be here to lead them aboard. I will take my leave then. I was merely wishing my son luck on his journey."

"That will be not be necessary, my dear. You'll be accompanying him."

The stag gave pause, confused. "Um, my Lady, it is typically tradition for the parents to stay behind, is it not?"

"Indeed, Bomeran. You must have noticed the cargo within the fur of my tail, and I'm sure you heard the news of what had happened to their father?" as she spoke this, her face appeared a bit forlorn. She was trying to keep her demeanor without breaking out into tears as she started to speak of the tragedy that befell her family again.

Bomeran looked down somberly. "Quite, I'm sorry for your loss, he was a good spirit."

"As are you, which is why you are coming along on this journey: these little ones need undivided attention, as does being a Sage; I cannot do both."

There was a bit of a silence, then suddenly something seemed to click and Bomeran seemed a bit taken aback. "I-I understand, I'm honored, my Lady! I'll pack some things at once." Garoo blinked a bit as his father had rarely ever stuttered, it was so uncharacteristic of him to do so that he felt as if he probably had finally fallen asleep and was merely hallucinating such a passage of events. He had never heard of an adult coming on this trip, and he wasn't quite sure what it meant, but it obviously took his father by surprise.

Garoo watched the elder buck as he worked his way back through the crowd. The young kangaroo was confused, "He seemed kind of excited by the prospect of watching over your kids while you perform your duties, never seen him behave that way."

The rodent gave a laugh. "Oh… I'm afraid you—" she was interrupted as the liquid in the bay began to become unsettled, signifying the large ship's approach. "You'll learn a bit later, for now, I've got to get everyone ready." She smiled and gave a bit of a bow to the kangaroo. Garoo loosened his tail's grip around the dock post as he returned the gesture—the Sage's presence had cleared some space and he felt less claustrophobic.

Standing before the crowd, the squirrel Sage looked upon the masses and spoke. "May those to be blessed with the gift of the Powers, whose spirits have grown to be big enough to be chosen by them, please step forward and away from the comforts of childhood so that we may enter the responsibility of adulthood. May the Powers watch over us in this time of—"

The Lady's monologue was interrupted by the loud thunk of one of her little ones as they fell out of her tail to land on the dock below.

"Oh! Are you okay, sweetie?" She turned and picked up the little one and cradled it in her arms. The creatures watching smiled, some trying to hold back snickers, as they knew the child was okay, but the scene really broke the seriousness of the moment.

As soon as the squirrel had the child in her arms, she looked up to see the others on the dock simply looking upon her. She flushed a bit with embarrassment. "I'm sorry..." she apologized. The child in her arms looked out at the crowd with blissful lack of awareness of the scene he had caused for his mother.

Bomeran had arrived back on the dock with a small satchel containing necessary travel belongings. The boat was set up and the boarding ramp had been deployed. With that, Lady Wollnutt could see they were ready to go. "I suppose we shouldn't hold up too much longer, time is short and we have far to travel. Please make an orderly line and follow me."

The water outside the cabin area churned as Garoo found an empty bunk to set some of his belongings under. He tended to travel lightly when he made the rare occasion to—this journey was no exception. While he wouldn't need his own place to sleep as they were scheduled to arrive at their destination before nightfall, each person on board got their own bedding and chest to put any belongings into.

As the kangaroo was placing his last item into the compartment he was suddenly startled as he felt a paw grab his tail from behind. At first he was alarmed that it was Fangstro come to beat on him again, however, after a few non-violent and playful tugs, he realized he was not in any ordeal.

"Ding, ding, ding!" came Kareen's voice from behind, to which Garoo closed the chest and turned his eyes to the otter as she wriggled his tail with a grin.

"Hey there, what's going on?" he asked as he stood up and looked over his shoulder giving his tail a wiggle in return in kind of an odd form of handshake before the appendage finally slipped from her grip.

She frowned a bit as she placed her now empty paws to her side. "Nothing much, Urand got a queasy feeling in his stomach as soon as we left the dock, he's now up on the deck, probably losing his breakfast."

"Lovely…" Garoo gave a shake of his head as he was quick to switch topics as to not remind himself that he was also a bit nauseous. The topic that was on his mind wasn't any less easy on the nerves, as he was still concerned over her being offended when he left her to fend for herself the night prior. "Look, Kareen, about last night."

"What about it?" the otter asked in a nonchalant manner.

Her tone clearly made it already clear that she wasn't really bothered by what had occurred as much as he thought she was. "Eh... forget it."

"Already way ahead of you," she said with a laugh.

Garoo gave a smile in return as he spun around and sat on the bunk, his tail hanging over the side of the mattress. "Great."

There was a pause in the conversation, creating a bit of dead air. The cabin was relatively large and held many bunks. The space was shared by pretty much all the occupants with exception of the crew and some of the very important individuals, such as Lady Wollnutt, who got their own private quarters.

At that moment Kareen thought of something that had sparked her curiosity earlier: "Oh, I thought I saw your dad come on board at the dock. What was that all about? I thought adults who were already affiliated with an element didn't come on this trip."

"Oh, that?" Garoo shrugs a bit. "It seemed the Lady wished him to come along to help her out with her kids or something."

The otter thought a bit and then put her paws on her hips, elbows out to the side. "Haha, really? I somehow doubt that, if she wanted help with her kids it would have been easier to leave them back in town with him wouldn't it?"Garoo tilted his head his ear flopping to the side a bit. "That makes sense I suppose... the Lady said she needed help, I didn't exactly catch with what exactly."

There was a bit of a pause and then the otter's face lit up a bit. "You don't suppose, that she's going to resign her position as a Sage to your father do you?"

As she asked that question everything just seemed to click, and the kangaroo felt like a dunce as he fell back into the bed as he laughed. "Oh wow, why didn't I think of that? This lack of sleep thing must be really getting to me!" he exclaimed, the news was quite grand indeed and changed a lot about the possibilities of his future. "This is incredible, I mean, I'm so proud of him! No wonder he was acting so odd this morning."

The otter sat on the bed next to him. "Are you going to be okay?"

He sat up, a bit somber. "It's just a bit of a shock to me is all, I mean the son of an Elder is one thing. But the son of a Sage? It is a bit much to take in. That also means we're not going to have as much time before he passes on the position to someone else."

Kareen blinked and then sighed, "Yeah... great... here I thought maybe... we'd just have a little time before all that. Depending on what happens it'll be you or I and either way. I still don't think it's fair that he has us competing for this, this ritual will determine the rest of our lives, should he really be treating it as some sort of game?"

Garoo sat back up. "I don't think he's treating it as a game as much as he just isn't sure which one of us he wants to lead, so he's letting the ritual determine which one of us the Powers choose as the better individual to leave in charge."

The otter stood up with a yawn, she couldn't stay in the bed too long as there were still things to do before the end of the day and just sitting upon the bunk was making her tired. Thinking of how her brother kept her up all night made her wonder how he was doing with his nausea, "I think maybe we should check how Urand is faring. Probably make sure his breakfast was the only thing he has tossed overboard."

The roo sat up and put a paw to his tan stomach. "Urk! Could you refrain from talking about such things? I'm not doing all that well myself."

As the two wandered out of the cabin and Kareen griped about how she had to grow up in a village of landlubbers, a muzzle perked up over a nearby bunk. The creature had been lurking in the shadow throughout the conversation. Only after the two had left did Fangstro's sister, Sharlean, reveal herself. She had to go tell her brother about what she had just heard as she knew it would be of some interest to him.

The wolf moved out of the large bunk room to the hall and went down the stairwell into the belly of the ship. Even on a vessel as well kept as the Arcane, the moisture in the lower decks gave a bit of a musty flavor to the air. She had finally made her way back to the main cargo hold, the place where her brother had told her he and his friends were going. Her eyes adjusted to the room's dim light as she entered.

Fangstro sat on the sturdiest crate, his subjects around brought him the spoils of their raids of the shipments. He sat there with an arrogant smile, as if they were truly his gifts to digest and not those for the keepers of the temple and the residents nearby. As he bit into what was harvested a bit of its inner juices flowed down his muzzle. Truly nothing tasted better than knowing that one day he would have the best; just like those in the temple did. He then noticed that his sister had entered the room to which he gave a smile as he picked up a glass mug which was filled with a beige colored liquid. "Ah, did you change your mind and come to enjoy the fruits of our labor?" he asked.

"Our parents are the ones who picked those crops, and they are meant for the keepers at the Omnigic Temple and the Sages," she replied. While she typically followed her brother, she was still her own spirit. Sharlean still respected those in authority, unlike Fangstro. She did habitually help her brother give Garoo a hard time, but this was not for any delight. She believed that Garoo needed to be harassed, for in a position of leadership he needed to be strong, and, as her brother repeatedly showed, the kangaroo was weak.

"Come to lecture me then, my little sister? I thought you said you would leave us and head back to your bunk." Her brother glanced over to her with glassy eyes, clearly one of his age was not really supposed to partake in the liquid he currently ingested.

"I did, however I had overheard a conversation between Garoo and Kareen regarding the Eldership of Emergant. They said something about Bomeran making the decision that it'll be determined by the Powers, and depending on if they favor Garoo or Kareen, he'll give the position to one of them. If Garoo fails, it'll be going to Kareen," Sharlean told her brother.

Her brother's calm and joyous demeanor shattered and, with it, the glass he once held in his paw. After he threw the mug of liquid, it flew over the head of a colleague and hit the bulkhead with a crash, startling everyone in the room. His nose was still sore from the previous night's punch to the muzzle that the otter had gifted him, and the thought of her becoming the Elder had dumped salt upon the pride's open wound.

"That shrew?!" he exclaimed as his voice deepened; a bitterness to his very breath. "What does she have that I don't? She obviously sees something in that meek mutt of a kangabuck, and those that see value in the feeble must also be themselves! This position was supposed to be ours' sister! Our family's! Just because our father died before we were old enough doesn't mean we should be forced to forfeit it!" he growled and then leaned back into his throne of crates, letting the turn of events come to a boil as thoughts of what to do next simmered within.

As the wolf sat his upper lip curled a bit as he let out a deep growl. His claws raked into the wood of his impromptu chair, carving out claw marks into the material. "It's hypocritical!" He exclaimed. "He says 'let the Powers choose' yet he limits their choices to simply those two? I'm sure the Powers will see me as far more worthy than that lot! Yet I will still be seen as inferior to Bomeran? So in the end is he really letting them choose or himself?" he pounded his paw into the crate. The sound of the impact on the hollowed object echoed around the hold. "The arrogance!"

His sister gave a thought. "Well, you may be correct, however it is possible that Bomeran could select another should neither Kareen nor Garoo be seen in favor. I've never seen a forsaken become an Elder, so if they both happen to come out of this without an element then I wouldn't see why Bomeran wouldn't select another."

There was a bit of a silence as Fangstro processed her words, and then he jumped up in a jubilation. "Sister of mine! That is exactly what will happen! I shall see to it that it happens!"

Sharlean was a bit confused by that remark. "How are you going to do that? There is no way to fathom what influences the Powers. What makes you think you can do so?"

In the shades of the cargo hold the white teeth of her brother glimmered in the dim light as he spoke. "Oh, it's quite simple. I'm going to make sure neither the weak mutt nor that otter will be able to make it to the ritual. I will be sure to disrupt their prayers and block their ability to consult with the Powers. Then, neither of them would be entrusted with what should have been ours!"

His behavior, his instance and hatred for the two truly was frightening, and even to his blood relative. She was hesitant. While she was behind her brother during their youth, and their treatment of Garoo, she actually did have some admiration for Kareen and never saw her as a weak link. Clearly her brother was no longer caring about the future of their kind, instead he only seemed to be care about himself and his own legacy—so much so that he was talking of physically disrupting a ritual of their people. She had respect for their traditions, and seeing all this, she could no longer go along with her sibling. "I'm sorry brother, but I will not be helping you in this matter."

The posse and its leader all turned to her, as if she had grown an alien appendage that made her appearance in the room in its own way an oddity. Some of the members had a look of disbelief, with some anger and fear mixed in, knowing that the disagreement between these two could make things rather ugly. All they could do now is brace themselves for what was to come.

"What?" the male wolf stood up from his crate and walked up to his sister, glaring upon her as he stood before her. "You'd allow those two to shame our family like that? Are you just as weak as they? They should be stopped! Our village will crumble under their leadership."

She frowned. "You're telling me the Powers would allow someone who's truly weak to obtain power to surpass yours? You seem to think so, because you are trying to get involved in their decisions! Who is the arrogant one brother? You would defy our traditions to stop them? You would defy the Powers' ability to choose to make your own?"

The male wolf raised his paw up, ready to bear down. His own sister dared to defy him? To question his word? He felt ready to strike, however there was still a bit in him that hesitated. His sister had helped him throughout his childhood and was still family. Fangstro lowered his readied attack and instead went over to a stack of crates and gave a good, solid kick. As the stack clattered to the ground, he refuted. "I'm not overriding the Powers. The Powers chose me to be here, and they guided me to make this decision. Should they have not wished for me to do so, then you wouldn't have sent me this message. Clearly they want me to stop this! If you have no wish to do so, then just get out of my way! I'll handle it myself."

He felt the anger and disbelief that his sister would stand against him about to boil over. He knew he had to leave the room before he did something he really did not wish to do, so he moved past her. The posse started to get up and leave as well, one by one moving around her and through the door, each with different flavors of glances as they moved on by. Some seemed sympathetic, while others appeared to burn with anger, and some just tried to avoid eye contact altogether as if simply wishing to try and keep their head down from this sudden divide in the siblings' stances.

Sharlean let out a sigh; she sort of felt responsible for her brother's behavior now and throughout their childhood. The canine carefully moved past the downed stack of boxes and made her way to the crate throne. As she sat down, she ran a paw along the gauges left within the material. Her mind wrestled within as to whether she should try to warn someone of her brother's intent. Right now, she just wanted to keep her head down. Perhaps her words were enough to reach him and he wouldn't actually go through with his plan.

Bomeran stood within the door frame leading into the more luxurious cabin accommodated to Lady Wollnutt. Her room was one of the best-furnished on the ship, surpassing even the captain's quarters, as it was garnished with an overall green theme symbolic of the Sage's element of land. The Lady was looking about the room as a servant finished tidying up the space. Wollnutt's children were now out of her tail and were instead playing in a corner that had toys strewn about.

After the initial shock of the Lady's message to him, his head started to think more clearly once again and something just seemed off about the reasoning behind the Sage's request. He was here to inquire about the concerns he had and though the prospect of questioning a Sage made him nervous, he felt he owed his people to know the full story about what he was getting himself into.

The Elder cleared his throat so that his presence would be known to those in the room. "Excuse me, my Lady, I wished to speak with you about something. Is now a bad time?" he asked with a bow of his head.

Wollnutt spun around, she gave the Elder a smile "Oh, Bomeran, not at all my dear." The squirrel turned to her helper and dismissed them. "Thank you very much for all your help. I can handle the rest from here."

As the servant moved toward the door, the buck moved away from the doorway so she could make her leave. While there was a moment of silence the squirrel walked about the room, moving amongst the potted plants and blooms of flowers that aligned the bulkhead. She grasped upon a red petal of one of the flora and caressed it to check upon its overall health before sighing contently. "I will miss a few things about this position. They always made this arrangement for me when I go upon these trips to the temple. It's really like having my own little floating garden and it makes me feel at peace."

With a nod the buck replied and got right to the issue bothering him, "They are lovely, but it does make me a bit curious. Why are you resigning from your position? I know you told me it was for the sake of your children, but in your position you could simply arrange for another to look after them while you were in the midst of your duties. I mean no offense on your wishes, my Lady; I just feel that there is something more to it. Is there something else that is bothering you?"

Her paw released the petal and she gave her head a shake and looked down, she gave another sigh, this one less content than the one she had given earlier. "Well, it is fortunate that my last decision as a Sage was a wise one at least. Your ability to see beyond the surface shows that you are up to the task." She moved over to a table in one of the corners of the room and pulled a chair out inviting the buck to sit down. "Have a seat and I shall tell you. However, what we discuss here cannot leave here, it would do the public no service to divulge in the story I am going to share. As a Sage you're going to hold a lot of burden, and you will have to become used to its company. Are you sure you wish to hear this?"

"Even if it's not easy to hear, it's still better to make decisions when fully aware of the circumstances," the buck responded as he took a seat at the table.

"Very wise," the squirrel replied as she sat at the other end of the table, she reached under her seat and placed a thin wooden rectangular box upon the table, a pair of metallic hooks kept the item locked within a folded position. As her paws unlatched the hooks she was able to open up the object from the center, which became apparent as to be some type of gaming board. She asked her guest a question. "Are you familiar with the game of Lament?"

Bomeran quirked a brow as he turned to the folded object. "The Sage's game? I am familiar with it."

She unfolded the board and set it upon the table. "It's called Lament because it is a game that symbolizes the conflicts of old, when the elements fought amongst one another in their petty feuds like in the tales. As the Sages play the game, so the world does lament, for agreement and harmony gives way to bickering and feuds. The game was meant to settle these feuds without violence, though sadly the result of the competition doesn't always result in peace."

The squirrel took out a pouch and dumped the contents upon the table, pieces to be placed upon the board that was opened. The game arena consisted of two six by twelve rectangles that were perpendicular and conjoined at the center, forming a cross with equal extruding lengths. Of the playing pieces, there were four different colors which were representative of their respective elements: crimson for fire, cyan for the air, dark blue for water, and of course a forest green color for land. She aligned the pieces to each side of the board, one for each element.

"The idea behind the game is that each Sage plays their own element, they are always set up directly across from the opposing element. Fire sets up across from water, ground from air. However, it is important to note that one's opponent is not always the same from game to game. In fact, fire and water could face off against land and air in a two on two game. It all depends on what the dispute the game is settling."

Bomeran looked up. "So basically one side of a debate plays against the other?"

She nodded. "Correct, though you'll come to find that there aren't always two sides, sometimes there could be three different views and there will be three teams, uneven of course. Sometimes, which I've never had happen, all four could have a completely different view and it becomes a free for all, sometimes an element might decide to sit out if they have no opinion in the matter leaving their pieces dormant." She tried to find the words to further explain, giving a pause, before conceding. "Talking only does so much, we should start by playing.

I'll take the air pieces. You can take the land. To make this simple, we'll just leave fire and water dormant." The squirrel turned the board with the dark green pieces facing the buck and the cyan ones facing herself.

The Elder paid attention as the squirrel explained the rules of the game, she explained what each piece was and the importance of them working together to accomplish their goal, she started by moving her own piece and then explaining some strategies, Bomeran grasped the concepts relatively quickly as he had always been a quick study. "So has there been a lot of conflict among the Sages lately?" he asked curiously as he moved his pieces toward the center of the board.

With a sigh and nod, the squirrel made her move, the game continued and the conversation advanced to the conflicts that had gripped over the elements. After the Tri-Societal War had died down the four seemed to return to their bitter feuds they had before they had united during those difficult times.

The squirrel eventually told the story of how the Sage of Fire had brought to the council's attention that she was having a feud with her life companion, but this was more than a simple lover's quarrel. He had started to commit raids against her towns and supply caravans. As the ground dominion relied heavily on those land based trade routes, Wollnutt gladly was willing to spare some resources to deal with the rouge mate. More importantly though, was that Lady Wollnutt and Lady Pardinia were good friends, and she knew personally about the troubles she was going through.

The fire mage was very stubborn and didn't want to bring relationship issues before the council, so to do so required a lot of effort on her part. The other two mages of water and air stood against their wishes. The Sage of Air was a stubborn politician who cared for traditions and the old ways, and was quick to return to them after the war had ended. The Sage of Water was, to put it lightly, very unwilling to do anything that had required risk, and though water mages would have proved very useful against rebel fire users, he declined.

Lament was played, and the female Sages lost against the males, unfortunately the leader of the winds was well versed in the game, and typically got what he wanted, almost to the point of monopoly, a position he had grown a bit fond of over the years.

"That is why I am resigning more than anything, I feel I am letting down my people and my friends. I am not very good at this game. I'm sorry you have to learn from someone as lacking as I, but it seems you are already doing quite well," she complimented.

"To be honest, I kind of looked into the game, just in case. I know it's sort of taboo for lower mages to learn the game until a Sage passes it on. However, I had found some ways to obtain some of the knowledge for myself," he confessed.

At first, the squirrel frowned a bit, but then shook her head with a smile. "Well, despite the unorthodox course of your actions, I think these times call for a little bit of gumption, perhaps your boldness will be enough to tip the scales in the land's favor."

"I suppose so," Bomeran smiled as he moved his piece to its awaiting square, to which there was a sudden pause.

"Well, hrmm..." the squirrel's tail fluffed as she pondered at the puzzling predicament her pieces now lay in. After a few moments passed, an object suddenly came crashing onto the board from across the room knocking the pieces off the board and scattering them upon the wooden floor. The culprit was a ball which was knocked into the air by one of the Lady's offspring. Whether the action was purposeful or accidental was unknown, however, what could be concluded was that this particular game was now over.

They both looked over to the youth as he looked back, worried he was going to get in trouble. "Sometimes life has ways of hindering even the best laid-out plans," Bomeran concluded, a bit upset since he felt he was in control of the board at that moment.

"Indeed it does," the Sage responded.

The adolescents had gathered on the upper deck. It was a nice day outside—the clouds in the sky were sparse and the warmth of the day washed over the crowd. They were far enough out of the bay where no feral birds could be seen overhead. This gathering was not a spontaneous act, they had all gathered to be taken on a tour. Of course, most already knew of most of the important locations on the ship already so this escapade was not to explore the vessel but instead to discover the future that lay ahead, and recount the past that led them here.

A form looked down upon the group from his position on a balcony that looked over the deck. The crowd looked up at him as his presence was realized, easily recognizable because of his shorter stature. If he had been down amongst the group below he could have easily had been lost from sight. The deep blue of his justaucorps complemented his deep green skin.

With a nervous croak, the frog Sage of Water looked upon the large group. He hated crowds, and really wished he could go crawl in a mud hole somewhere. The only companion he had ever wanted was the sea, and it was probably only because he was in her presence that he could even bare to have all these younger forms looking up at him. However, his mind turned toward the fact that this tour would have them go below deck. He pictured the squeezing of bodies down narrow corridors. He could see the taller creatures of the group. He could see the walls tightening, the group pressed into him and trampling his shorter form.

These fearful thoughts solidified his desire not to go through with this. If only Lady Wollnutt were here then he could let her lead them through. "But where is she?" he wondered aloud.

"Who?" a voice came from behind the frog causing him to turn around and face the back of the ship.

The frog recognized the voice as the elderly owl figure with many titles. His official one was Wiseman Strig, a historian whose age made him almost just as historic as the tales he told. His other titles more aligned with his eccentricities and were spoken mostly by the youth who felt his skewed personality odd. Titles such as "Old man Strig" or "Crazy Old Strig" were common ones. His feathering patterns were a bit faded in color, mostly a pale tan with some darker spots here and there.

His startled jump had the short amphibian turned around to face the owl. "Would you kindly not sneak up on me like that?"

"Hoot-" The elder avian tilted his head to the side. "Those that are easily startled tend to have the largest burdens to hide," he proclaimed before repeating his question. "So you were wondering where someone was? Who?"

The Sage of Water heard past the ending question of who he was asking about, believing it was merely a part of the owl's dialect rather than an actual question. He looked over to see some of the crew looking toward him from their positions on the bridge, he felt oddly naked with the owl's plain insight, one that might have hit a bit close to home. This only made those curious glances seem more menacing than they actually were. "My alleged burdens would be none of your concern even if I had any of them, old man," his tone was a stern, as he had to keep some image of backbone, probably to make up for the fact he wasn't much known for having one.

However, the owl remained persistent in getting his question answered. He didn't even seem the slightest bit deterred by the bit of agitation in the Sage's voice. "You didn't answer my question. Who?"

"What are you talking about? I didn't hear a question in there," he said, still confused.

"Who? That's what I asked you. Who?"

"What did you ask me?"

A bit agitated, the owl fluffed up his feathers and shook his head bit in sort of a twitch. He had realized finally what was tripping up the Water Sage: mistaking questions for hoots happened to him far too often. He cleared his throat as his feathers started to go back to a more natural position, "I was asking about the particular individual you were complaining about not being here at the present time."

The frog turned back to the group of youth gathered below as he sighed a bit. "Oh, well, Lady Wollnutt, she was supposed to be here to help me with this tour."

"Hoo—I believe the lady is with company in her quarters at this moment. She will not be needed, though, as I wish to do this task myself. I feel I have not much longer in this world and I always wanted to have the honor of teaching aboard the Arcane."

With a croak, the frog turned back to the elderly owl, "What? That's—" his tone started off a bit confrontational before it had cut off, about to lecture on how irregular that would be. However, the opportunity of being able to skate being trapped below deck with a large crowd was far too tempting an offer to not accept. He stepped away from the balcony as he made his way back toward his cabin. "You know what? Knock yourself out," the frog said as he moved away, leaving the group to the old creature.

Meanwhile Garoo, Urand, and Kareen were standing by the starboard edge of the deck as the other passengers started to gather. Urand's color was starting to return to him as he felt much lighter after losing the weight of his morning's nourishment.

"Feeling better?" Kareen asked her brother as she ran a paw over his back, to which the bear gave a nod.

His stomach gave a growl. "This may sound funny, but I'm feeling hungry now."

Garoo gave a bit of a laugh. "I'd say he's doing better," he said with a smile. The kangaroo was thankful that he was starting to feel less nauseous himself. Perhaps it was the fresh air doing him good, or it was the fact that his stomach didn't have contents to empty, seeing as he hadn't eaten anything of substance in a day. He winced a bit as his stomach reverberated and reminded him of this fact.

Behind the group a wolf stalked them in the crowd, moving toward them. Fangstro stood behind them for now, not bringing attention to his presence. His grin bore a nefarious scheme, the signs of a predator waiting for the right moment to strike its prey.

As the chaos of conversations continued on deck, some noticed an older creature make his way down from the bridge. With a spread of his wings, the old owl got the attention of any in the group who were distracted, "Hoo-Hoo!" his voice called out as the tips of his wings spread to the sky. "Listen here, all of those who journey to adulthood."

Conversations on the deck started to die off, some quickly and respectfully while others stubbornly clung on for dear life. Those were eventually stifled by impatient individuals who beat out the side talk with grunts, clearing throats and awkward stares. It was particularly awkward as the owl stood there, wings agape in awkward silence, waiting patiently for the eventual attention of all before him.

After he was respected with silence, the owl started his discussion. "I, Wiseman Strig, am here to pass the wisdom you shall need to understand the path before you. We approach the shores and, when we arrive, you shall make your way up to the Omnigic temple: our holiest of holy temples. In there, you will become gifted in the element that is your destiny."

He lowered one wing and pointed the other to the sky. "If the Powers care, they may gift you with air." The wind blew as if on cue, tugging upon the sails and, looking above, the youth could see some additional avian creatures were up in the crowsnest, their wings glowed a light cyan which were barely visible against the morning sky as they directed the winds to the sails. "Hoot! As one can clearly see, every gift has a role, on this ship the mages of wind keep us on course and make sure the winds always are at our backs. They are our bards, or word carriers, and our scouts."

"Should they decide a different stand, the Powers may give you the power over land." His wings showed a group of creatures on the crew who Garoo recognized from their province, mostly creatures of the forest. "Now you may think these mages are useless out here on the seas with no land to draw from. However, look to your feet and you shall see that the essence is still beneath it. The trees, while dead, still can be manipulated by the mages. Their magic can make them as tough as any metal of this world."

The owl then moved over to dark colored canisters that lined the outside rim of the deck and pointed out to the ocean beyond. "Or should the Powers desire, you will be gifted with the power of fire. They are forgers and craftsman, but on the ships they man the ballistic weaponry." As an example a fox placed a ball into the cannon and then placed his paw on the back of it. His paws glowed red, and he focused, causing a contained explosion to expel the projectile from the front. Some of the crowd gave a startled jump at the sound, while others gave out approving audio cues giving unsubtle hints that the element surely had new fans.

"If none of these powers are in destiny's jotter, perhaps instead you'll yield the power of water," the owl proclaimed.

Urand took the opportunity to tease the rhyming and whispered over to his friends. "More than likely if your species is an otter."

Though she was typically fond her brother's joking behavior, she found herself a bit annoyed because this was the element that she wanted to hear about. That, and it was a bit rude given how old and respected the teacher seemed to be. She glared at Urand and gave the bear a hush as the owl continued his lecture. "I'm trying to listen," she whispered harshly.

Perhaps a bit too harshly—a whooping "Hoo!" got everyone's attention as the owl had paused his monologue. The feathers of the creature ruffled a bit as he peered over toward the otter and her company. "Is there something the matter over there? Does your future bore you so much? Please share with us: what things could be of greater importance?"

Kareen lowered her head in embarrassment as she was scolded and was about to apologize on the group's behalf when Garoo chimed in. "Well, we had heard that sometimes the powers do not bestow someone with an element at all. Is this true?"

With that question, the old creature's face changed from one of agitation to one a bit more somber. "Indeed this is true, young roo. Do you fear that the Powers not look with favor on you?"

"Well—"

The wolf that had been shadowing and waiting for an opportunity to damage Garoo now grinned as he saw an opportunity present itself. Before the kangaroo could answer the question, Fangstro injected, "He has doubts about the Powers! I heard him say that just yesterday."

There was a bit of shocked silence that permeated for a long minute on deck. Then a trickle of background conversation became almost a torrent of crosstalk. The weight of such a charge was heavy indeed. To be a doubter could easily lead to ostracisation at best, being treated as a traitor and prosecution at the worst. Garoo felt the crowd's talking and staring becoming a thick and bitter soup of vitriol. He felt most of them seemed to be staring at him with disbelief, disappointment, some maybe even anger.

Before the crowd became too unruly, the owl spoke up. "Silence! Be still, younglings!" the Wiseman squawked. The seas of conversation calmed and order had been restored and as things returned to normal. The old creature turned to the kangaroo. "Does he speak the truth?"

Garoo felt himself tense up, the whole thing had made him feel a deep weight in his chest. He could lie, perhaps, to make things easy. Lying just always made him feel rotten on the inside, however, never had the consequences of telling the truth been so dire.

"Well?" the owl pushed for an answer.

With a sigh, the kangaroo decided to try and explain how he truly felt, for he did not have much practice in deception it might be worse for him if he tried to hide it and people were suspicious of him. He looked up to the older bird. "I do have doubts about how we perceive the world around us. I think those flaws can sometimes extend to those beings outside this world as well. I don't—"

Before his enemy could finish, the wolf injected again. "He admits to doubting them! He should not be permitted to enter our most holy sanctum!" he decried. Fangstro put on a faux look of disgust, but he knew what he was doing. If he could keep Garoo from even being allowed into the temple then he would never have a chance to be anything in society, no less an elder. His words already had an impact as the crosstalk started up again, there were some cheers of agreement that could be heard amongst the group while others were not quite sure.

Garoo closed his eyes and let out a chuff. Despite what was going on he had to finish. He raised his voice a bit to repeat the last sentence. "I don't doubt that there are powers beyond our understanding, which is why I doubt when people claim they understand them. I don't doubt them, I doubt us."

There was a pause as the owl looked over the young tan creature as he finished his words. The ears of the younger being moving back, ready for the consequences of his word and anticipating the worst. Kareen in the midst of this was giving the wolf who had started the whole charade a death glare.

After what seemed like an eternity for Garoo, the owl finally spoke. "Hoo—He is not a doubter. He doubts mortals; there is a difference. Also remember that some of our greatest prophets who asked the powers for proof when contacted by them. Did not the camel wandering the desert ask the guardian of fire to prove herself? Did she not show him evidence of her presence by burning a nearby shrubbery? If this kangaroo had committed a transgression by questioning the brothers and sisters of flesh and blood, then would not Fillard the Camel's transgression have been worse by questioning the deity directly?"

Conversations began to buzz again as many people thought over these words, many respecting the wisdom in them, others trying to wrap their head around such a concept. For some that were told that questioning the Powers was treasonous, they weren't used to having highly-praised figures spoken in such a light. Then again, the owl was truthful; the story of Fillard was a well-known one in their history.

Thankfully for Garoo, the older creature's words were enough to get the crowd to calm down. The owl let the talking fade on its own this time. He knew that it was important that the words he spoke were absorbed into the crowd via their own thoughts rather than by him just forcing it upon them. As soon as it quieted down enough he decided to go ahead and answer the original question asked.

"Any hoo—to answer your question roo: if none of the elements the Powers feel you can partake in, then you shall forever be seen by our kind as forsaken." The owl somberly looked over to a small group of ship assistants that, until this point, had gone unnoticed. Compared to the mages shown to them earlier, the attire these creatures wore was much simpler. Some of them started to notice that they were being stared upon, which they weren't used to, and some of their faces showed their disdain for the gawking as they went about their tasks.

"Creatures have different ways of dealing with the forlorn. Some treat them with empathy, some with pity, while others treat them with scorn. They can be found spread throughout the provinces and are typically given tasks requiring more grueling labor. During the war, many of them were put on the front lines and were usually the ones to take the most casualties. They are fortunately few, but these few are the ones the Powers decree are to sacrifice the most."

One of the forsaken seemed to be oblivious to the conversation taking place and continued their task of swabbing the deck. Garoo watched him as they went about his duty. His appearance alone told a story of hardship. He wore a tattered plain colored rag which was printed with the stains of his necessary but thankless tasks. His fur was tattered from the sweat and grime of his labors, while others seemed to have other marking indicating more permanent scars. The kangaroo really felt himself hoping that those had been obtained by accident and not by purposeful cruelty.

As the roo perused the less fortunate crew members the owl inquired if there were any further questions that people would want to have answered before they moved on. Urand rose his paw, much to his sister's fear as she gave a worrying look that her brother was about to embarrass her.

"You seem to constantly talk in rhyme. Why do you do that all the time?" the bear asked. There was a bit of a snickering heard. Others were a bit silent as the question seemed to them kind of offensive to be asking to those of a more regal age. Kareen put a paw up to her furred forehead and rubbed. She thought she was surely going to have a headache.

The owl was quite surprised by the question. "Oh! Well, that's simply a 'bad' habit of mine I suppose. You see, I hail from the air province and we tend to have a thing for storytelling, particularly in the form of ballad, as I alluded to earlier. So sometimes we can be a bit stuck and rhyme our words even when we don't aim to."

"Any further questions?" Wiseman Strig asked his audience. There was a bit of a pause, the last question was rather bold and was a bit difficult to follow. "Well if that's all let us—"

"Couldn't we just have the water mages help with cleaning the ships decks? Why do we have those without elemental gifts do it?" Garoo wondered aloud.

"Putting yourself in their shoes wimp? Don't worry, you'll be there soon enough," Fangstro jibbed. Kareen gave him an icy glare in return. She was getting agitated at his smugness. "These lowlifes are considered cursed by the Powers, it should only be fitting that you feel as one of them."

"And you think the forsaken will be motivated to come back into their good graces when their followers are treating them this way?" Garoo shot back.

This kind of arguing was sifting into the crowd. The divide was there, too. Those from the aquatic province were more apt to look at the forsaken as slaves, while those from the forests didn't view them quite as low. Fangstro was, of course, an exception not only because he wanted to get Garoo in bad graces with his peers and the Powers, but also because he was always one to assert his authority over those who had none.

The owl interrupted the disagreements with a loud screech. "Order young ones… worrisome is your bickering, it reflects those found within our ancestors."

"Then tell that kangaroo that he's wrong!" came a voice from the crowd that did not belong to the bitter wolf.

With a sigh, the owl shook his head. "I cannot place a stake in the future. My duties are simply to inform you of the past, the Sages are the only ones who have authority to try and shift our path." He turns from the crowd. "Please follow me, and I shall show you the fruits of our ancestor's feuds."

The teacher made his way toward a wooden door, swung it open, and revealed a stairwell that went below deck. At most they could file down two by two following him down. Garoo and Urand were the first two, Fangstro managed to keep behind the kangaroo, moving down next to Kareen. The otter held her breath, keeping an eye on the wolf as she tried her best to hold back her resentment of the creature in such close quarters.

Unfortunately for Garoo, the depth of the wooden planks of the stairwell was not large enough to support his full foot length. He had to move carefully as he alternated one foot over the other, stepping a bit sideways to keep himself from tripping over his own feet. As the wolf noted how slow the kangaroo was navigating the stairs, he found his patience running thin. It got to the point where Fangstro really felt like pushing him out of the way.

With that thought, the canine grinned. That might be just the ticket to get Garoo into trouble since the owl was just ahead of the kangaroo. If he stumbled into the older creature it would really make him look bad and maybe even get him punished in some way. Even if that wasn't the case, he might be injured enough so that he wouldn't be able to go through with the trials ahead.

As the large-footed creature went to carefully plant his next step, the wolf gave him a jarring push from behind. Kareen immediately saw what the wolf had done and it made her livid. She spontaneously slammed the canine into the wooden bulkhead, which caused everyone behind them to stop and try to break it up. Some noticed the roo making his unnatural descent down the stairs, letting out worried calls and alerts to the old owl Strig that he was in danger.

Despite his age, Strig's hearing was keen and he quickly spread his wings and flew down the rest of the steps to avoid the body that was tumbling toward him. As the owl reached the bottom of the stairwell, he sent a blast of air to push against the falling kangaroo to slow his final descent at the foot of the stairs.

As Strig had just about had enough, he let out a loud screech, and spread his wings. A gust of wind rushed up the stairs and caused Kareen to stumble from her grapple. "Break it up! Get down here this instant!" the old owl shouted up to the group. He turned to the kangaroo and offered and wing to help him up. "Are you alright, young one?"

Garoo gripped the extended appendage and used the help to get back onto his feet. A bit of soreness took hold as he felt some bruising on his right elbow and along his thighs but nothing felt broken. "I don't feel too badly injured. Thanks," he said as he started to move his limbs to make sure they could function properly.

The rest of the creatures gathered at the foot of the stairs. Kareen was still glaring at the wolf as he kept a worried eye on her. His nose was still a bit stuffed from the bloody nose she gave him the night prior, and he really didn't want another one. The owl moved towards the wolf and otter, his feathers puffed up on his chest, clearly upset. Kareen's glance moved away from Fangstro and over to Strig's angered expression. Her own bitterness faded away as she felt the elderly owl stare holes into her.

"I understand that the debate on deck was intense, but we certainly don't have time for this nonsense!" he leered at the otter as he spoke. "Young lady, it pains me to do this, but I'm going to have to ask you to return to your quarters until we make shore."

Kareen looked shocked as her nubbed ears leaned back. "Me?" she asked in a bit of disbelief.

"Of course you," the owl hooted back. "Your roughhousing on the stairwell could have done more damage than it had. There are many wonderful artifacts down here and I don't want them to see them tumbling to the floor as our dear kangaroo has."

"I did not cause Garoo to fall, the wolf had pushed him!" She looked over to Fangstro as she made her accusation.

Strig looked over to the wolf. "Does she speak the truth?"

"I don't know what she's talking about, she just suddenly lunged at me and caused me to stumble a bit. I might have accidentally bumped into the kangaroo during the struggle, but I didn't purposefully push him," the dark wolf said with a helpless look.

"You're such a liar!" Kareen spat, her eyes going back to a glare, cursing that she couldn't hit him with all these people watching and with her under such suspicions.

The wise owl turned to the crowd and started to inquire as to what had happened. Unfortunately, most of those behind the otter and wolf had not seen the kangaroo get shoved. The first thing they noticed was when Kareen had slammed the wolf into the wall. None of them actually saw Garoo get shoved.

"I did feel a shove from behind..." the kangaroo noted.

Strig gave a nod. "We know that you were shoved, what we're unsure of right now is how this shove occurred." He gave a sigh. "We don't have time to thoroughly investigate this now, so I stand by my decision. I, as a simple creature, can only go by what I have seen, and that is that the young lady was the aggressor and so it is she I must ask to leave."

"I'm right here, you know!" Kareen sighed, annoyed that she was being talked about like she wasn't present. "Forget it, I'm out of here… let me know if I missed anything of actual importance," she huffed as she moved through the group back towards the stairwell trying to keep herself from breaking down into tears over being falsely accused of being the aggressor.

Garoo waited a moment, wondering if it would be proper for him to follow her or not or if he should stay as was expected of him. Urand wasn't going to wait around though and dwell on it, though, so he quickly made his way up to follow his sister to the upper deck. As everyone had turned to watch her leave, Fangstro gave a grin. That had gone a lot better than he had hoped.

Kareen had stopped at a railing on her way back to the passenger quarters and looked out upon the expansive sea. She had always wanted to be on a ship like this, but now she felt it as a prison surrounded by the water she loved so much. Whenever she was stressed, she'd usually go for a swim, but with how fast the ship was moving she could not. It was vexing to be surrounded by water and not be able to do anything but just look at it. The only water she was able to touch was the stream that started to drizzle down from her eye.

"Sis!" Urand called out to his sibling as he had come up behind her.

The otter was startled a bit as she wiped away the tear and cleared her throat. "U-Urand," she stammered a bit. She turned around partially to her brother to keep her sorrow hidden. "Aren't you supposed to be with the others?"

"I was worried 'bout you sis," the bear replied. "Are you alright?"

She gripped her paw on the railing as she shook her head, facing back toward the ocean as she shook a bit. "It… just makes me mad. He won't stand up for himself!"

"You know that isn't his way, sis. He doesn't fight, even if he should, he doesn't."

The otter sighed, "I do know this, but every time I stick up for him I get in trouble, or Garoo gets upset with me, I'm sick of it! I'm just sick of it." She slid down and sat by the railing, her paws running up to her muzzle and up through the fur, tugging it a bit in stress. She looked up to see Urand was alone. "He didn't even follow you here, I mean, is he even worried about me or does he think I was the cause of him falling down the stairs? What does it say when even he doesn't believe in me?"

Urand knelt before his sister and looked down to her. "I don't think he doesn't believe you sis, he just doesn't take sides unless he knows the truth. I'm sure he believes Fangstro did what he did, he just can't prove otherwise, so he's not going to cause a ruckus over it."

"Well, I know a way to fix that issue," she glared. "If he won't stand up for me, I won't stand up for him. Tell him

I don't want to see him, at least not until this trip is over. I don't want to ruin my chances by being kicked out of the temple and being ostracized to defend someone who doesn't want to defend himself."

The bear looked a bit saddened by that statement. He wanted to defend his friend and tell his sister that she was taking this a bit too far, however, when his sister had her mind made up, it was sometimes best to just stand down and let things play out. "Alright sis, I'll let him know."

# Chapter 3
# The Town of Omnigic

The group moved through the underbelly of the ship. While the lighting was rather dim, the contents of the lower hold were still rather drawing to the eye. Images of artistry and collections of culture lined along the walls in organized groups. Along the side of the wall was a mural which stretched over the bulkhead for scores of feet, highlighted with lantern light. As they made their way down the wall and observed the artistry, the owl guiding them narrated.

"In the beginning, there were Four and they were One, unified in harmony, despite their differences. They brought peace, happiness, and balance to the world and the creatures who followed them prospered. They were Grountis, the giant elk whose humongous antlers branched like the towering oaks of the lands he looked over; Stratis, the golden eagle whose spirit soared across the skies and whose plumage shined down on the world like a star; Ignitis, the sabretooth whose teeth were as sharper than the finest of swords and whose red coat flickered like the purest flame; and Aquatis, the archelon whose massive shell carried the lost and weary over the sea of turmoil in life.

"As time moved forward, those who worshipped the Four as one started to grow apart. The creatures that had been gifted with the powers of the elements began to become selfish and full of pride for their particular One. Verbal disputes turned to violent overthrows.

"The Powers were not pleased by this showmanship. They were not happy that their followers were separating themselves as they still believed the Four should be one, so the Four punished them by creating enemies that would bring turmoil and hardship unto them. This marked the beginning of the Tri-Societal War."

They moved onto the next part of the long wall art, which had taken a turn for the dark in contrast with the peaceful beginnings. There were dark silhouettes of a more tribal and barbaric looking culture with sharper looking features. These interlopers flowed into the painting becoming more and more prevalent as they moved further down the work. The owl continued his narration, "We called them Farawlz, and they were the first race we had encountered outside our own culture. Primitive beings who normally consist of creatures who lack any form of fur coat. Some of them look reptilian; others insectoid. They have no belief in the Four, they only believe in one principal and that is that survival is the proof of one's worth.

"Although not being magical beings, they were still a formidable foe. Their skills are inherent by birth, not given by rite. They used these inborn skills to survive and defeat their opponents. Despite the diversity of their society and species, there seemed to be three main principles that kept them united as a race. The first was strength, which allowed them to win in physical melees easily against the other creatures of the world and allowed them to survive against aggressors. The second was swiftness, which was important for those who lacked strength, as sometimes finding clever ways to carry oneself in a fight or avoid death was also a means to survive. The final pillar of the Farawlz is fertility, which ensured their race—while not having magic or technology to hide behind—had the numbers to replace those whom were lost."

As they moved along, the mural took a strange turn; the chaotic nature of the more tribal creatures transitioned to a society which was very ordered and structured. There were many objects that weren't recognizable to the youth in the room. There were mostly grey and metallic colors. Tall structures placed together in village like communes and metallic constructs which roamed over the land and into the sky. There was a barrenness to it and a notable lack of any natural-looking elements.

Strig went on to explain this transition in art style. "Though the Farawlz were persistent and a tough opponent to be sure, it was the third race involved in the war that truly were our greatest rivals, the Domistechs. Unlike the other primitive race, the society behind this race is advanced as the technology they wielded. They lived in large groups within forests made of metals and glass. These creatures cared nothing for the Powers and instead manipulated the world around them with their cunning to create their own gifts.

"Their society was complex so I couldn't do justice in explaining them in great detail. They were comprised mostly of rodents, canines and felines who were not fit to survive without their technology. They tinkered with the world in unnatural ways. Despite this, they did have some diversity—particularly they convinced some of the lowlier in our society to convert to their ways.

"Dishonorable in combat, they mostly used their advanced technologies to hide their relatively frail forms. Their metal beasts ranged from treaded turtles that traversed the terrain to screeching flyers which soared the skies. So, despite their lower population, they were able to prolong the life they did have."

As the owl continued his monologue, there were some audible yawns within the crowd. Fangstro became impatient. "Who cares about them? We won right? Why dwell on such have-beens?"

His feathers fluffed a bit at the sudden outburst. Were all youth of this generation so disrespectful as to interrupt an elder's lessons? "Well if you allowed me to conclude you would have known that despite having beaten them, our rivals still exist on this planet of ours. The Domistechs seemed to have gone into seclusion at the conclusion of our last victory, their metal forests as dead as the materials used to construct them, abandoned. The Farawlz have become fractured and prone to extensive in-fighting, so they are hardly seen attacking us anymore."

As Garoo looked over the large image on the wall, he thought aloud back to a question he had pondered the previous night with Kareen. "They looked rather formidable, how could we have overcome them? How did we make them lose the will to fight?"

"Well I'm sure the fact they were doubters had something to do with it. Advice you should heed yourself, long ears," Fangstro jibbed.

Garoo's kind of interruption was more welcome to the avian creature. Strig ignored the wolf's presumptuous answer and decided to tell what he could about it, which unfortunately wasn't much. "Well, I'm glad you asked young one. Unfortunately, that is a day of which we do not speak."

A familiar voice came out of the crowd. "Well, if we aren't supposed to speak of the-day-of-which-we-can't-speak, isn't saying we can't speak of it speaking of it?"

The kangaroo couldn't help but chuckle as he realized that Urand must have returned from checking up on Kareen.

The wise owl gave a bit of a grin, too, as he responded. "I'm not speaking of that which shouldn't be spoken of. Instead, I'm merely referring to the event as one which I cannot detail."

There was a pause before the bear countered. "But we're still speaking of it."

"Hoo!" String decided to put an end to the tangent. "Let's just say we were victorious and leave it at that. In our victory we did lose something, which is why we tend not to discuss it."

Garoo continued to pry, "Is what we lost of consequence to us? I think we'd be entitled to know."

Though the owl's gaze started at the roo, his eyes seemed to shift toward Fangstro as he spoke. "The impact of what was lost has already been made. For some of you, the effect was greater than others. How much consequence that effect will have on the future has yet to be seen."

Urand gave a rub to his head. "Do you always answer questions in such perplexing ways?"

"Hoo—I am only answering the question I am asked. Perhaps they merely reflect the complexity of the inquiry."

The bear paused before shaking his head. "Forget I asked."

With a grin, the owl feigned memory lapse. "Forget what now?" he teased as he went back to the current topic.

"Anyways, after that day the war had quieted down. Many of you were born at this time, or just before, so you were too young to comprehend. The Tri-Societal war had ended and you'll be the first generation to not have a memory of its horror, a blessing for certain. One that you'll no doubt take for granted. Anyways, let's move on to our next item of interest."

As their guide began to move, Garoo moved over toward where Urand who was near the back of the group. "How is she?" he asked the bear.

"Sis? She's pretty mad. Says she wants to be alone 'til the end of our ritual. She's afraid of gettin' kicked out before she can enter the temple. She don't wanna defend you if you won't defend yourself, especially if it's gonna get her in 'ta trouble."

The kangaroo sighed, "I never asked her to defend me. It's her temper that got her into trouble, not me."

Urand gave a frown in response, "Now listen here, Garoo. We're buds but my sis attacked him because he attacked you. I think sis feels you need someone lookin' out for you since you won't look out for yourself. I don't think this is easy on her so I'll keep her company and she'll probably calm down. But I'd keep away from her until this trip is over."

"I know. Once she's made up her mind, it's best not to argue it too much. I don't like it though, I feel as if everyone just wants me to be something I am not."

Before the bear could respond to his friend the group had reached their destination. The group had stopped before a table which was dressed with a fancy red fabric, an elaborate wooden rack placed upon it. What was within the holder, however, seemed oddly misplaced. The owl picked it up and presented it to the youth.

"A fishing rod?" came a grumble from the dark wolf.

"Yes. What is wrong with a fishing rod? Being able to catch food is a very important skill to have for any creature. I mean, no one is interested in starving, are you?"

"We all know this old man, I thought we were talking about the trials that made our people strong!" Fangstro complained.

"This is true. However, when war is all said and done and there is no one left to fight, then of what use is a weapon?" the owl hooted. "This question is rhetorical of course, our people had already asked and answered that for ourselves. Our society, unlike the other races, does not create weapons for the sake of being such. Most of our weapons have some form of peaceful application."

There was a bit of a pause and then a boastful laugh as the dark wolf again commented on the item before them. "You're pulling our legs old man! You expect us to believe we defeated our enemies using fishing poles?"

The owl retorted slyly. "Well was it not you who called them weak have-beens? If this is the case, then surely we could have dispatched them with a rod, correct? This particular instrument was used by a legendary Water Sage who died early on during the Tri-Societal war. We kept his weapon here."

After they realized the owl was serious, the group became perplexed. The owl played a little bit more with the rod, letting the confusion take hold before he flipped the pole upside-down so the end of it was facing upwards. "You see, appearances can be deceiving!" he declared. After a click, the butt of the pole separated from the rest of the rod. A metallic song was heard as the blade of a long, thin sword slid out from its unique sheath.

The owl moved the weapon about the air as the group let out utterances of surprise, then returned the weapon into the benign-looking fishing instrument. "There are many benefits to having the tools of our livelihood also act as weapons. It keeps them at the ready, it encourages their maintenance in more peaceful times, and of course it can catch one's opponent off guard."

The guide placed the rod back into its rack and went to move to the next item. "Anyway, now let's—" the elderly avian was interrupted by a loud ringing of a large bell from up on deck. He looked disappointed, knowing what that sound meant. "You ask too many questions and now we are out of time. There was so much more to cover, yet we are now approaching the shore. Please head back up and get ready to depart, your destiny awaits you."

With those words, the youth dispersed. While some did find the tour of interest, most were thankful to leave the aged teacher. Their interest clearly laid more in the future before them than in the past behind them.

The large vessel arrived at the port. It was most certainly a different perspective looking down upon the village from the deck than looking up to the ship from the dock. Though usually the more humble sort, Garoo felt like his large feet could step upon the smaller forms below as he walked down the passenger ramp. The village seemed so miniscule in relation to the galley they departed.

"Makes ya feel like a capital-dweller doesn't it?" Urand joked as he followed the roo down to the dock below.

Compared to the village where he grew up, the small size of this Omnigic Valley town certainly did make the kangaroo feel as if he'd lived a comparatively privileged, capital-city-like life. While its location lay directly between the four major provinces and its proximity to their most holy temple should have made this a popular point to settle for their race, many factors kept the town's size so small.

Excepting the quadrennial pilgrimages when the water was calmed, the sea surround the port was too rough, making the town difficult to access by water. From the north the only real access was by foot through mountain tunnels. Turbulent winds from the northwest were just as unforgiving to air travelers as the waves could be to visiting sailors. The wild forests to the south were particularly hazardous, overgrown by vicious plant life and crawling with aggressive non-sentient creatures. Only the most foolish would attempt to traverse it.

Of course, accessibility was only half of the issue. Being in the center of four unique biomes which made up each province, the central hub had very bizarre weather patterns, as if the Four would battle over their dominance over the holy center. Sometimes Ignitis would bring heat and drought, and then Aquatis would return with a vengeance bringing downpours and flooding. At their worst, these events refused to yield to the magic of even the Sages themselves, truly leaving the people here at the mercy of the Powers. To live out here made the natives into survivors. Despite the harshness, it was important that people remained to defend and maintain the temple grounds. They had to be frugal with their resources, as farming the land to forage their own was difficult because of the adverse weather.

After they were on solid ground, Garoo looked around for Kareen. Though he knew she didn't want to see him, he still worried for her. "Yeah, it is quite isolated, isn't it?" he said, talking just as much about how he felt the otter must be feeling right now as much as the town itself. "Urand, could you do me a favor?"

The bear peered up to the kangaroo, "Yeah?"

"Could you look for your sister and make sure she's okay? I mean, my father is here, though we're friends and I know you worry about me, it's just—I don't want her to be alone. I think she needs you more than I do."

"Are you sure? Sis can handle herself, ya know."

"I'm sure. I've seen her cross before, but this is the first time she has refused my company outright. I just worry I—forget it, you're right I'm underestimat—"

Garoo was interrupted when his friend put a paw on his shoulder. "Hey, if it makes you more at ease, I'll keep an eye on her for you. You sure you'll be okay though?"

The kangaroo gave a nod. "Yes, I'll be fine. Thank you."

"Alright then, I'll see you after this is all over, then we can go showing off our new abilities and causing all sorts of trouble." The bear ran off to go find his sibling.

"Me? Cause trouble? How long have we been friends now?" he shouted after him as the bear disappeared into the dispersing crowd. Without hearing a response, the kangaroo smiled and shook his head as he moved down the edge of the dock.

Luckily for Garoo, his father was relatively easy to find in a crowd with his large yet asymmetric rack, not to mention that he was still hanging around Lady Wollnutt. They had congregated around the open cargo hold as the crew unloaded the supplies. Because of the uneasy seas, the only major trade that occurred with the town in Omnigic Valley was during the Day of Transition when the pilgrims settled. This was why the Sages used the Arcane not only to transport the youth to the temple, but also to attempt to supply the residents for the next four year period.

As he got closer, the kangaroo could hear a pretty heated conversation going on as a resident stood over one of the crates that appeared burglarized. The scent of the ruined fruit's juices was pungent and covered up the scents of those nearby. The Lady spoke calmly despite the obvious insult inflected in the voice of the recipient. "It is clear that one of our passengers had been less than hospitable when it comes to our traditions," she said, keeping her children close by to assure they didn't hinder the crew from offloading.

The local was livid, "Never in my many years of service have I ever seen such a blatant disregard for the offering to us! We stay here to keep the temple safe and to repair it and all we ask is for our supplies to come to us unperturbed! Do you think the powers will look lightly upon this transgression?" as he asked the question he turned his ire to the kangaroo looking over toward them. "Mind your business! You come here to admire your work?"

Bomeran turned around to see who the resident was accusing. "That's my son, he's probably here because I'm standing here, and I don't believe him capable of such—"

"Of course you wouldn't. What are you doing here anyway?" The irate individual turned to the buck. "You don't look like you're part of the crew, you're not young enough to be part of the Transition, and you're certainly not a Sage."

Lady Wollnutt replied. "This is Bomeran; he is here on my accord. He did not touch your supplies either, for he was in my company for the duration of the trip."

The denizen was perturbed. "For what reason? Are we just not going to respect any tradition anymore?"

Bomeran looked back to the damaged crate. "From the looks of it, the damage was thankfully minimal. Since we don't know who the culprit is, we'll just take the punishment as a group. Perhaps we could agree to not have any festivities tonight."

Garoo's stomach growled as his father put forward that proposition. It was tradition for there to be another banquet after everyone had arrived—a second night of eating and celebration on the eve of heading up to the temple. Unfortunately for the kangaroo, his actions over the prior days had left him with little nourishment, so hearing he might lose another opportunity to eat was a kick to the stomach.

This proposition did calm down the resident though, "That would be more than fair. I'll present the possibility to the Elder when I speak with him about this. It certainly would make these kids realize what it means to rely on the gifts of others and to starve when those gifts are ruined." With that said, they returned to assisting the crew bringing the shipment to the town storage.

Lady Wollnutt smiled as she turned to Bomeran. "Indeed you are worthy of replacing me on the council. You handled that situation quite well."

The buck sighed, "I am certain those who are innocent of any wrongdoing in this case are not going to be so pleased at the resolution."

"I wouldn't doubt Fangstro was involved somehow," Garoo noted.

"Neither would I, son, but I really have no evidence to go on nor do we have the time to investigate this thoroughly. If it was Fangstro, however, I'm sure the punishment will make those who ally with him a bit agitated at the outcome of his decision."

The kangaroo's stomach growled. "Of course they got to eat, I haven't."

Bomeran nodded. "As you just heard, sometimes one needs to learn to go without for a little while, even if it isn't comfortable." As he spoke, he noticed that his son was alone. "Where are Urand and Kareen?"

"Well…"

The terrain was certainly unique in the Omnigic region. The village nestled on the east bank of the river that shaped the asymmetrical valley. While the east bank near the coast was traversable by foot due to the slope heading up to a ridge above the village, the west side of the river was not so easy to traverse. A rigid rift formed a cliff that cast its shadow upon the east in the afternoon light.

Kareen had come to see the temple for herself. She had traveled up the path to the east until the eastern slope turned into its own cliff forming a canyon. A waist-high cobblestone wall was placed at the edge of the east side to prevent people from stumbling to their death. Over the barrier she could see the Omnigic Temple, built within the western cliffs. The temple was built within the cliff face where a notch was carved out. The legends say it was naturally there when the founders had come. By how perfect the formation was, it was hard to believe such a crevice could occur by nature alone. Some more skeptical would probably claim it was by beast's paw, though most believed it was the Powers who left it as a placeholder for the building that would be made for them.

First they had built a stone bridge over from the more easily traversed east cliff over the river several scores of feet below. It wasn't a simple flat bridge, either; the crevice in the western cliff was a bit higher than the top of the eastern cliffs, so there were stairways on the bridge itself at intervals. Kareen could hardly fathom the difficulty of construction. It made her appreciate the works of those no longer amongst them.

"None of the stories hold a candle to seeing it in person." A voice she quickly recognized came from behind the otter.

"Urand?" she was a bit surprised to see her brother again. "Weren't you going to be keeping an eye on Garoo?"

The bear gave a hearty laugh. "He wanted me to keep an eye on you, actually. I can't duplicate myself, I can only watch over one of you at a time."

She turned back to looking across the ravine towards the temple, "I can take care of myself." Her eyes looked up to the top of the Sage's Tower, which rose high above the attached temple. At the top of the tower was the Sage's Chamber, signified from the outside by four large stained glass windows of each of the four elemental colors and illustrated with their own representing deity.

As the two gazed at the building, they didn't notice the wolf coming up the path and making their way toward the overlook. Fangstro had come to gaze upon the building for himself. Despite its regal presence, he did notice Garoo's friends standing at the stone railing. He looked about quickly and found a boulder to hide himself behind as their conversation continued.

Kareen glanced over her shoulder toward her brother. "So I suppose you told Garoo that I don't want to see him until this is over with?"

"I did deliver that message, yes," Urand stated. "He was worried about you. To tell the truth, so am I. Is there something wrong?"

The otter leaned against the stone barrier with a sigh. "Things are just too important right now, brother. I need all of my focus on the trail ahead and I cannot do that and protect Garoo at the same time. When I see him in trouble, I don't hesitate. When the actions I take could jeopardize my entire future, then I just need to keep my distance. He's not by himself is he?"

"No; he's with Bomeran righ-"

There was a loud ringing the echoed through the air up from village in the valley below. The sound was instantly recognized by the pair as a call for them to return to the town square. Each town had these meeting bells which were usually used in emergencies. This time its use was planned as a way to get all the newly arrived guests to the town on the same page before they went to the temple in the morning.

"Must be the others from the fire and wind provinces have arrived," Urand noted.

The otter gave a nod as she stood up and turned to start up down the path, "We should get heading back then. Don't want to be seen as tardy and get into further trouble."

As the two made their way back toward the village, Fangstro chose to remain hidden. Though he thought of maybe trying to hinder Kareen from getting back in time for the meeting, he knew such a conflict would not end well for him, as he was outnumbered and he had to get to the gathering himself.

Despite not being able to hinder her directly, the information he had heard was vital. With Kareen keeping Garoo at a distance during the Transition, he could certainly make easy work of them by widening the gap between the two. After the otter and bear had moved far enough away, the wolf headed back for the town himself. He needed time to scheme and come up with a plan to take advantage of this new confidence.

The announced cancellation of the celebratory dinner was not taken too well. The arrivals from the fire and wind provinces were particularly livid as there was no possible way for them to have damaged the Arcane's cargo. After the unfortunate gathering had drawn to a close, Fangstro's peers were also rather perturbed, particularly at the creature who had led them into theft of the goods in the first place. They waited until the crowd dispersed and crept outside the village to assure they could speak freely and unheard.

With an arrogant smirk the wolf wrote off the negative criticisms and purported his mistake as intentional. "I knew the celebration would have been called off. It's all part of my plan."

"What plan is that? For us to starve? For everyone to get mad at us?" came a voice of dissent.

With a confident laugh, Fangstro waved his paw dismissively. "They don't know it was us. Besides, they'll be starving more than us since we already ate today. Garoo and Kareen have not, they'll be distracted by hunger. Besides I have stowed away extra—"

He stopped in the middle of his sentence as his eyes fell upon a purple-petaled plant growing off the side of the path. The wolf grinned wide as he moved toward the flowering bud. There was a spark within his storming mind which erupted a brush fire of self-appraisal at his blundering craftiness.

The others looked to their leader in confusion as he started to walk away from them and toward the flower of interest. "—boss?"

"Well! Isn't this convenient?" the wolf grinned. He slid his paw below the plant's sepal before beheading it of its indigo petals.

One of Fangstro's lackeys was clueless as to their leader's intent. "Uh, we may be 'ungry but I wouldn't eat dat dere plant boss. It'd knock ya out."

"I know that, you dolt! It's all a part of my plan!"

After a pause for thought, it was clear that there was still some confusion: "How is knockin' yourself out part of the plan?"

A smacking sound cracked through the air as the wolf's paw met the poor fool's muzzle. "It's for Garoo, you stupid—" the dark canine barked, then took some deep breaths to calm himself. He pulled out a satchel and opened it to reveal some of the stolen rations from the ship that he had tucked away. Fangstro crushed the bulb in his paw, rubbing the pollen against the food. Its fragrance was as soft as warm bedding, which is what made the plant so notorious for such tricks. The victim wouldn't suspect a thing. "The kangaroo hasn't eaten anything in the past day and I'm sure he's going to be pretty hungry, so I decided maybe we should give him a little gift."

He placed the tainted food back into the satchel and implanted a note indicating the rations were from the target's father before passing it on to one of his comrades. "Place this on the bunk Garoo is sleeping in. That should handle the kangaroo. Now go!"

"Right away!" the accomplice made off with the package in paw toward the guest house, where all the visiting creatures slept.

With that plan in motion, all Fangstro had to do was figure out a way to take care of the otter. It would be a bit more difficult, seeing as her brother was going to be hanging around. He would not be able to sleep tonight; he needed to somehow stop Kareen without being noticed.

While the fire of the sky had burned bright all day, its time alight had faded rather quickly. The long and stubborn night had returned to the land. It seemed that Garoo had waited his whole life for this day and, now that it had arrived, things seemed to go by quickly—making a part of him wish there were some more time to prepare. All the same, there he was, outside the bunkhouse where he would spend the night, with his father standing beside him.

"Well, this is where we'll be parting ways for the night, son," Bomeran informed the roo.

"You're not staying in the guesthouse?"

The buck shook his head. "I'm to report to the Chamber of Sages at the temple. Lady Wollnutt has arranged me to meet with the other Sages and to get acquainted. I'll be spending a good portion of the night there." He placed a hoof upon his son's shoulder. "The next time we meet, you'll be an adult. Your mother would be proud…"

Garoo noted that his father's words sounded a bit distant at the end. He wondered, "Is there something the matter, dad?"

"Yes, actually, but it isn't something I will talk about in the open air. I did promise myself that I would tell you about it when you grew up." He looked into the bunkhouse as he removed his hoof. "I had a note delivered to your bunk when we had first gotten here. It concerns your mother and who she was. I figured since you are now grown that you have earned knowing the truth."

"What do you mean by that? What haven't you told me about her?" Garoo asked with concern.

"Just read what I wrote and know that it is the truth. Don't take it too hard that I didn't tell you when you were younger; I didn't want that being held against you by yourself or others and I still don't." He gave his son a hug before his departure. "Good night son, Powers be with you tomorrow."

"May they be with you, too."

The deer departed, heading back to the awaiting Land Sage, and Garoo made his way into the bunkhouse. Some beds already had sleepers in them that had turned in for the night, mostly faces he did not recognize. Probably most were from the fire and wind provinces who didn't get to spend most of their journey on a ship.

A few rows later and the kangaroo found his own bunk, the highest on a stack of three. He climbed up the ladder on the side and pulled back the sheet to find the letter his father had mentioned laying next to a satchel that he had failed to mention. As Garoo picked up the letter, he instantly recognized the signature as his father's, however, the seal that was holding it closed appeared to be broken. That was certainly strange, but at the moment the roo was more curious as to the contents than as to why the message was improperly sealed.

He crawled into the bed and opened up the satchel, his stomach immediately reacting to the sight of the ripe piece of fruit which lay at the bottom. His father must have left him a snack to enjoy with his reading. Knowing that the others in the room were also probably a bit hungry he slid himself under the covers as not attract attention as he started to read the letter.

**Dearest son,**

**What I am about to tell you is a secret about your mother only a pawful of individuals know about. Under a sense of**

*respect toward our family these creatures chose not to share this information with others carelessly. I would also advise that you keep this to yourself as well, however I share this secret with you now because I feel you have the right to know, being her son in blood.*

*When I first met your mother, I had just been given a plot of land by my father as a gift. My mother had also given me a gift and that was a worker to help me work the plot I was given.*

As he continued to read along, the kangaroo took a bite out of the fruit.

*The slave worker my mother had given me, like most in our culture forced to work, had no power over any of the elements. However as the years went by and we endured the labors of working the land together I had come to realize she had power over something much more—my heart.*

*You see, the worker was...*

Garoo began to feel himself struggle, having to read and reread parts of the letter.

*You see, the worker was my first life companion...*

The kangaroo strained to focus his eyes. The drowsiness had come out of nowhere.

*... my first life companion. Your mother...*

His head bobbed and he became distant for a moment as the written words seemed to blur. He relocated the words and dragged his eyes forward.

**Your mother, she was a forsaken.**

That was the last word he had managed before unconsciousness took hold and the kangaroo collapsed onto the sheets in a deep sleep.

Few were ever blessed with the privilege of entering the Chamber of Sages. The trip up the tower's spiral staircase was certainly a grueling one, but it was certainly worth the effort. Looking upon the room after the long laborious climb felt like looking down the peak of a mountain at the majesty below.

The spacious room took up the entire girth of the octagonal tower. Every other wall had a sprawling stained glass window that almost took up the whole area from floor to ceiling. Each window contained a representation of the element's deity surrounded by a background of their shade and faced in the direction of the respective province. Bomeran could only imagine how the light of day would shine through the colored glass. It would probably flood the room with their distinct hues. However, even under the warm light of the chandelier hanging from the flying buttresses near the ceiling, they were awe-inspiring.

While the four looked outside to their lands, they also faced inside toward the room's center where a lone table stood. Bomeran found himself drawn toward it; upon the surface he saw a game board. By the placing of spaces and the placement of the pieces it was easily recognized as a lament board. The peculiar thing about this particular board was that the pieces all seemed to be made of some sort of colorless glass making them indistinct from one another.

"How are you supposed to tell which pieces are whose?" Bomeran asked of the Land Sage.

She followed the deer over toward the table and went to sit down. "Oh, well, here: I'll show you."

As she sat down she closed her eyes and seemed to concentrate her energies toward the board. The shade of the pieces on her side started to shift in shade and glow a rich green tone. "The board can detect the element of the Sage, we move using the energy gifted to us. Try to move one over there physically with your hoof."

When Bomeran moved to the other end of the table and did as the squirrel instructed. He found that despite his best efforts, he was unable to move the piece.

"It's impossible to physically move them, one must use the Powers' gifts," Lady Wollnutt explained as she stood back up, the green tint flowing out of her pieces until they were colorless once again.

"Showing him how our little game works, Lady?" asked a new voice whose sudden presence had startled the squirrel. The lynx had grinned at the two as she approached, her smile enhanced by the tufts of fur upon her cheeks. "You woodlanders startle far too easily."

The Land Sage took the insult lightly as she took the moment to introduce the newcomer. The lynx's sharp, feline teeth reflected the firelight, but her grin was neither hungry nor malicious: merely a teasing type of friendly. She wore a similar dress to Lady Wollnutt, only it stood out far more to the eye with its deep red hue than the soothing forest green the squirrel wore. Her ears bore her breed's signature strands of black fur jutting off the tips.

"I believe I told you about Lady Pardinia?"

Bomeran bowed his head, as was the custom. "An honor, my Lady."

"Such formalities! Just call me Pardinia." She waves off the buck's traditional gesture. "I may be a Sage, that doesn't mean I'm better than everyone."

Another voice joined the group taking advantage of that opening. "You most certainly aren't," said a deep voice followed by a screech. This caused Bomeran to look around the room, from wall to wall, searching for the source of the new voice. He then noticed that the others were looking up. As the buck followed their gaze, he noticed a silhouette standing in the shadows cast by the buttresses holding up the chandelier.

As the form spread its wings to descend to his peers, the lynx didn't skip a beat in returning the insult. "Well you, Sir Sagacid, aren't everyone, so I can say for certain I at least come in above yourself."

The newly arrived Sage was now plainly visible as a falcon, whose wings were tipped with deep blue feathers and whose orange-tinted chest plumage was sprinkled with dark spots. Unfortunately, the beautiful coloration did sort of clash with his element's light cyan sleeveless robe. With a shake of his head, he quipped. "You would think that you'd show some proper manners with an outsider in the chamber."

"Our guest is going to be a Sage soon enough, so he may as well know what he's in for," the feline retorted.

Lady Wollnutt cut in before the bitterness between the two took too much hold. "This is Sir Sagacid of the Wind Province. He's been the eldest Sage for many passings now."

"Indeed. It is with a heavy heart that I must know it is you who will be leaving our order, Lady Wollnutt." He reached out a wing to grasp the underside of the squirrel's paw and rested the other wing lightly atop. "You truly are a proper Lady, unlike others who are given that title."

The feline could easily hear the falcon's passive-aggressive tone directed at her through his faux charms. Again, though, she immediately swung the attack back toward the bird. "Really, you shouldn't see yourself in such low esteem, 'Lady' Sagacid."

Releasing the Land Sage's paw, the hawk turned himself to face Bomeran, not even giving her the gift of a leering glance. "You'll have to forgive the cat. She's merely upset that we are not going to be wasting our resources on her little lover's quarrel. Quite frankly, I can't be too surprised that she and her life companion would have a falling out."

This statement elicited a hiss from the lynx. "Damn you! That's none of his business, he was not a Sage at the time those matters were discussed!"

"Well—what were your words? He's going to be a Sage soon enough, so he may as well know what he's in for."

The desert cat had her ears pinned back, a heat could be felt emanating from around her as she gave a glare in the bird's direction. It felt as if the fire in her heart might soon manifest itself into a more literal incarnation if this went on too much farther. Before the situation got much uglier, Lady Wollnutt decided to change the subject rather swiftly. "So has anyone seen Sir Anauran?" she asked, looking around for any signs of the frog Water Sage.

"Probably late, as per usual," the falcon replied as he simply went over to sit in an empty seat while they waited, knowing better than to push the lynx too much further.

"I was busy tending to the Arcane," a croak came from the chamber's entryway. The frog had a glassy look to his eye as he breathed heavily from his exhausting trip up the stairway.

The bird lifted his wings "Ah, there he is, we're honored you could show up, Hero of Bedell."

With a sigh, the amphibian approached the group.

Bomeran was a bit confused at the title. "Hero of Bedell?"

With a playful gasp, the falcon answered "My dear deer, have you not heard of the harrowing tale? Come, Anauran, tell us your exploits at the battle of Bedell."

The frog gave a croak of annoyance, he appeared a bit bothered by the topic. "There isn't much to tell."

"So modest! Why such a change in heart? When you first got here it was all you could talk about. How you and your crew were the only ones to survive in that devastating naval battle. How you took out a Domistech frigate. How the old Sage was lost in the battle, and that's why you were selected to replace him." The falcon's tone suggested he felt the tale was exaggerated. This was probably because, even to Bomeran, the frog didn't seem to present the confidence or bravery that would be required of such feats in the story.

"Well, I don't like concentrating on my past successes, lots of people died that day." The frog waved it off and looked to the deer. "This must be our new Land Sage? So what's your story?"

The other Sages looked to the buck, noting his asymmetric rack that sat upon his head. "Indeed, his is probably factual given that grave war wound," the lynx stated, indicating that she also had her doubts on the frog's tale of inheritance.

"What I saw… we don't speak of," Bomeran said with heavy words. Despite the cryptic nature of them, these words caused all present to become silent. It came as a total shock to all present (except for Lady Wollnutt) that Bomeran was present when the final blow of the Tri-Societal war was struck, and despite the taboo of speaking of it, at this high level in the society, they all knew exactly what that blow was.

The long drawn out silence was almost blissful to the squirrel. Rarely were these three in the same room without some sort of fuss or ruckus going on. "As you can see, I picked someone who's quite qualified for this job."

The fires of the morning returned again and the youth now waited in the main chamber of the temple. Prior to their arrival, each had placed their names upon a sheet of paper containing the order in which they wished to consult with each elemental deity. These papers would be placed in one of the corresponding four stacks, which would be drawn from when the respective elemental chamber was free for another to enter. Consulting with the powers was considered a private affair, so only one youth could enter each elemental chamber at a time. When they entered their respective shrine, the door would seal behind them. When it opened again the participant would either leave with that element's blessing, or as plain as they entered. If a youth came out without a blessing, their name would then go to the bottom stack of the next deity so that each adolescent would get up to four opportunities; one with each Power. If, by the end of consulting the four, they were still without an element, they would forever be forsaken.

Kareen was there, and was waiting to consult with Aquatis at his shrine. She was with her brother, who, instead of being nervous about the impending trial, seemed to be more concerned that he had not seen Garoo amongst the crowd in the temple.

"You're worrying too much, Urand. I'm sure he's fine." The otter wasn't sure if she was trying to calm her brother or convince herself by saying those words aloud.

The bear clearly wasn't convinced by his sister. He started to move away, looking amongst the strangers for his friend. "I should ask around. Maybe someone has seen him."

Before he could move too far, though, a monk walked out and called out amongst the room, cutting through the cross chatter. "Kareen. Aquatis! Kareen, to the shrine of Aquatis!"

With those words, the otter felt her stomach jump as she turned to her brother. "Here goes nothing. I'll see you when I get back," she said before walking through the crowd towards the water deity's chamber.

"Good luck sis, I'll be prayin' for ya!" he called after her before she made her way through the deep sea blue door, which closed with a clang behind her.

The room's lighting instantly became dimmer as Kareen was shut in. Lanterns hung at varying heights from the ceiling. Their deep blue, translucent, glass side panels caused the room to fill with a deep blue light which rippled along the stone walls. In the center of the room, there was a masterly crafted statue of the archelon Aquatis. A few stairs rose to a platform before the large turtle statue, clearly it was where she was meant to be when consulting the water archelon.

Kareen sat with her legs crossed upon the platform before the gaze of the imposing figure. She took a deep breath and meditated, trying to remain calm as she tried to focus and ask for the blessing of the seas.

The world around Garoo appeared to be hazy, as if that of a vision or dream but it was lucid and vivid. He was lying down, he felt swaying blades of grass tickle through his fur as he opened his eyes. Sitting up, he saw a peaceful field brightened by the day's light. The serene simplicity seemed to stretch to even beyond the horizons before him. Not a sound existed except the wind passing over the cusp of his ears.

The kangaroo stood and looked about the surreal expanse and then a new noise met his ear, causing him to turn to his right. He discovered the source: a pure white snake sliding through the green hues of the plain. Normally it was best to keep one's distance from such creatures, but there was something about this particular reptile that seemed to fascinate him. Perhaps it was the odd coloration, or that, as foreign as this creature was, there was something oddly familiar about it.

He continued to follow the slithering animal, simple curiosity leading him across the day-lit field to what appeared to be shadows that loomed ahead. The shade had an unnatural feel to it, as if the sky's fire were being blocked by some sort of body. The pale snake crossed over into the darkness, the slithering form stopping abruptly. Its passive hissing changed into a more aggressive tone, causing Garoo to stop in his tracks. The calmness of the day began to fade into the blackness of the shadow enveloping the ground before him, creeping up towards him as the serpent was. Garoo felt frozen. Fear took hold. The fangs of the snake bared and the creature lunged toward him with a quick flick.

A pained cry rung out as the antlered kangaroo shot up in bed, he panted to cool himself from the heat of adrenaline as he looked about the room. The illusion of his dream had vanished and had awoken him from his deep, pollen-induced slumber. He felt his head pound as his body regained consciousness.

As he looked about, he noticed the day's light peering through one of the windows at the far end of the bunkhouse. Any grogginess of the sudden rise was shaken as he recalled where he had to be. He cursed aloud as he hopped off the bed and hit the ground running toward the Omnigic Temple. He was late for the Transition!

As Kareen continued to meditate she felt herself begin to drift. A dripping sound started to echo within the aquatic deity's chamber. The sound of the water at first was not a hindrance to Kareen's concentration, but it started to get louder, until there was a loud cracking noise that shot her awake from her meditation. She jolted up as she noticed the large turtle statue leaking water from its eyes. The otter approached statue, feeling over the water as it trickled down, the dampness reaffirmed on her paws. The room started to feel damp as the loud noise of crumbling rock got louder and reverberated throughout the room. She looked around to see the stone walls start to come apart, water gushing into the crumbling structure of the room.

Before she had a chance to call out, the water crashed into the room, consuming everything, washing over her and surrounding her. She closed her eyes and held her breath as the rushing current threw her off her feet. When she reopened them she found herself surrounded by darkness of the depths which had filled the room. The light blue fires had seemed to transform into glowing jellyfish that moved about and provided light and what was the stone floor was now a coral reef.

It was at this point that she felt herself running out of breath. Her instincts had her looking for a way out in order to get some air. However she seemed to be too deep, while she started to swim up the only light in the area came from the jellyfish. She slowed down, just giving up, feeling she was going to drown.

There was then a large bellowing noise which caused her to spin around to see a large turtle which gave an ethereal glow as it flowed over head. The otter gasped at the sight, and it was at that point she realized that she could breathe. She instantly began to cough after having held her breath for so long, the sweet treat of air came as a shock despite being surrounded by water. She suddenly felt a calming rush of peace, being at one with the water, and no longer feeling it a threat to her, but really a part of her.

The kangaroo had made his way through the village easily; it had become like a ghost town. Everyone had gathered in the temple to oversee the ceremonies. He continued up the path, along the stone wall, and made his way across the expanse over the bridge. As he began to cross, he saw some silhouettes standing outside. This was odd; he thought everyone would be inside at this point but, sure enough, three figures seemed to be up to something at the temple's front wall. These figures seemed to notice his approach as well. "Someone's coming!" a lookout informed his group, who all immediately stopped what they were doing. A dark wolf climbed down from the wall to get a look at the interloper.

Fangstro growled loudly as the creature crossing the bridge became more clearly visible. "How in the depths did he wake up? There was enough pollen on that fruit to knock out a pawful of beings."

"What are we gonna do, boss?"

The wolf looked around and noticed that the coast was clear, he moved toward the other end of the bridge to block off the approaching roo from his destination. "We stop him from going in, of course."

"What about Kareen? She's entering the chamber and we need to stop her too!"

"I know that, you dolt! The kangaroo's a priority though," Fangstro decreed with a fire in his eye. His enemy was now in speaking range. Garoo was in such a hurry that he had almost barreled through them, but the wolf refused to budge.

"Where do you think you're going?" the canine growled.

Already flustered by his tardiness, the kangaroo frowned at the creature blocking his path. "Not now, Fangstro. You know where I'm going," Garoo said. As he tried to move around the group to their left, however, they shifted their position and kept him from crossing.

The wolf gave a toothy grin as he gave a gentle shove and said his next words. "Oh we can't let some spawn of a forsaken defile our sacred place with his presence now can we?"

While the push had temporarily stopped Garoo, it was those words that gave him pause. "What—How—How did you find out about that?"

"Ha! So it is true. One of my colleagues saw that letter on your bed. I couldn't believe it when he told me what was written on that rag, but now the truth is revealed right from your own mouth. Not that this truth is surprising in any way, shape, or form. Your mother was forsaken, and so are you by birth."

Garoo had had about enough. "That was not your letter to read and you had no right to it!" his voice declared sternly.

A burning rose in the wolf's chest as the kangaroo spoke to him with that newfound boldness. He felt as if he needed to respond, to not let such arrogance go unpunished. Especially not from some forsaken's spawn. "I read what I want, when I want! Now begone!"

Fangstro gave the roo a shove that was much harder than before, causing him to stumble backwards. As Garoo tried to plant his left foot down to maintain balance he felt his foot and heart sink as he felt no ground beneath his paw. Everything seemed to slow down as he started to tip, his body sliding from the bridge into the open air of the chasm being pulled down by gravity. He let out a cry for help, but by the time it had left his throat there was nothing that could have been done. The stone bridge flew up as he spiraled down.

The wolf and his posse ran forward to the edge of the bridge where the kangaroo once stood but now was gone. They looked down below to see where he had fallen, but the fog in the canyon was too thick and simply consumed any trace of his being.

Panic started to take hold as one of Fangstro's lackeys broke the silence. "Oh—oh Powers—boss what are we gonna do? Ya killed him! He's gone. We're gonna get it— we could be banished! We could be killed!"

It took a moment for it all to catch up to him, that Garoo's fall had actually happened. Once the grave reality hit, he snarled in frustration, swiping his hysterical comrade across the nose. "I know that! Don't you think I know that?" he yelled, himself trying to keep his cool despite this sudden predicament. He swallowed the panic and fear of consequence, almost shutting the act from his mind. "First, they aren't going to find him, so keep your mouths shut. Secondly, we still have to deal with Kareen..." he said going back to the original plan, as if nothing happened. "So hurry up and get me onto the wall."

After a moment of pause the others went back to Fangstro and pushed him up so he could climb the temple's wall. From there, he had learned, there were secondary access points to the chamber mostly used in temple maintenance by the residents. They would be abandoned during the ceremony. He knew he had to be quick though, as he didn't know when he would be called upon himself. Sidling along the notch in the wall, Fangstro crawled through an archway shaft that was enough to fit a creature. A light reflected off the wall ahead as the wolf made his way to the end of the tunnel.

It opened up to a large room with a bonfire in the center. Above the flickering flame was a deep blue stained glass ceiling. It was difficult to see through because of the bright light reflecting off of it, but he knew above was the shrine of Aquatis which was filled with the light from the fire before him. A stone stairwell gave him a secondary access to the room where the otter meditated. The dark wolf made his way past the warm light and headed up the stairs to the shrine.

As he made his way up into the main shrine from below, he saw his target. The otter was perfectly unaware of her surroundings in her deeply meditative state.

Kareen's body wriggled through the sporadically-lit darkness of the depths. She moved like a dolphin through the water, as if she had lived there her whole life. Her goal was simple and that was to approach the large turtle passing by overhead. She felt the need to go to the ethereal presence, that it was making her stronger the closer she was to it.

The distance between herself and Aquatis's form closed quickly. She felt the power of water starting to course through her veins, her ability to swim improved as she got closer and closer to her goal. Tears filled her eyes, this was actually happening; she was becoming everything she dreamed she'd be. Then there was a jolting tug and she felt the water around her echo her sudden change in momentum. Kareen wriggled and thrashed as she saw the turtle deity swim away and grow further in the distance. She tried with all her might to move forward but the mysterious grip held her in place. She looked down and saw these dark tendril like objects rise from the deep on her legs and holding her in place. She struggled in vain as one came up to wrap around her throat. Suddenly she felt like she were drowning again. She couldn't escape from the cold grasp around her throat.

In the shrine, the dark wolf grinned as he looked to the helpless otter, the one who had made a fool of him, had embarrassed him. His paws wrapped around her throat. Now she was alone, unconscious, no one would be able to stop him.

The anger in his heart and the fact he had already killed another made it easier on his conscience to not care about the consequences of his actions. It was so easy to take one life, so it was nothing to take the life of yet another. Actually, he thought fiercely to himself, if Kareen found out what had happened to Garoo, then who knows what she would do. It was kill or be killed. His paws wrapped tighter and tighter with each riling thought. In her trance, Kareen's breaths grew shallower while her body sank deeper into the depths.

# Chapter 4
# Birth of Light

Dust of decades long past hazed the air, making it heavy and hard to breathe. The only light to be found in this long forgotten room drifted from a newly-crafted hole within the ceiling. Unfortunately for the room's only occupant, he was the one to create that opening using very unsafe and unconventional means. The irony was that the painful forging of this new skylight through the old ceiling was just enough to make a majorly damaging fall not fatal for the roo.

Of course, as the kangaroo started to come around and his ears rung and his lungs filled with dust, it was hard to think of his fortunes as good. He coughed, slowly at first, but then throatier as he felt he had to relearn how to breathe. The torrent of hacking from his lungs finally settled down to let Garoo's mind wander to the shooting waves of pain that flowed over his body.

With his first few breaths and his heart racing, he called out for help. The only reply was from his own body as it called back with chest pain. He was silent for a moment, trying to stop the pounding of pain throughout his body as he looked up to the heavens through the hole in the ceiling his body had created.

There was a shift in the pile of stone rubble underneath him that forced him to move when he really didn't want to, he flipped onto paw and knee. During this involuntary motion he could tell he should not be moving of his own accord: he felt some bones not moving in ways they should have been. Though he screamed, he couldn't hear himself do so over the stab of pain that slammed his brain.

From his new position on his stomach he looked up into the darkness of the long-abandoned room. It appeared to be part of the temple, it looked like one of the shrine chambers but one that hasn't been entered in a very long time.

Even in his poor physical state, his eyes followed the streams of light beaming in from the collapsed ceiling, they fell upon a statue which towered high above the room. The shrine was the form of two snakes, one a pale snake with its maw open, sharp fangs bared to the world. The other was a more obsidian-colored snake, a calmer demeanor on its face. The two seemed to be entangled at the base of the shrine, their eyes peering at one another. From the appearance the light snake and dark snake were in battle with one another, though the darker reptile seemed to be a little bit less aggressive.

As the kangaroo slid over toward the shrine for some reason unknown even to himself, he felt tears flow down his cheeks. This was not how he had pictured his life to end, alone in this room. He at first felt sadness, but as a jolt of pain shot through his leg, the sorrow started to burn, it burned at the cosmos that conspired against him and put him where he was.

He looked to the shrine and he called out with his rasping breath. "So where are all the Powers? Where are they now when I need them? I'm supposed to meditate at these shrines to call upon them to help me, to give me their power. I don't want power, I just want to—to live." He used some of his remaining strength to pound his fist against the shrine's platform as he called out. "That's all I—"

An unexpected cough cut the roo's monologue, the creature bringing up his paw to cover his mouth. He pulled it away to see blood mixed with his saliva. The fluid dripped onto the shrine below, causing a sudden wind to blow throughout the room, whipping the roo's fur and causing him to close his eyes to protect himself from the particles kicked up into the air.

As things settled down there was a hissing noise which roused the kangaroo's ears to attention. "You poor creature," the new voice stated with empathy.

At first Garoo felt he was hallucinating as he looked up to see the form of an albino snake, thin and slender smiling a bit down at him, in what seemed to be a peaceful manner. "Wh—Who are you?"

The pale snake sat on the stairwell, "Name is Shadis, pleasure to meet you..." he surprised Garoo by reaching out to his shoulder with a claw, revealing the snake was not limbless. A chill ran through the kangaroo as the form's touch was cold, but also piercing.

"I see you've had a difficult time," Shadis hissed as he slid over to the front of the prone roo. "But I'm here to help, you asked for life. I'll give you that. But what good is life without purpose? Take my claw and we'll stand together."

In his current state, there certainly felt to be no other options. Garoo used his waning strength to reach and take the creature's offered limb. A chill ran through him and he found himself gaining strength and coming to his feet. The roo was about to thank him for helping, but the smile on his savior's face turned to a malicious grin, the grip tightening.

"I feel it in you, it's sssurprisingly light, but it's there," he hissed as a dark aura surrounded the clasped paws. "Let me draw it out, that power, feel it flow within you."

Garoo's mind was struck by visions, a darkness under his eyes as he saw physical manifestations of Fangstro and his posse. He was back on the bridge that he had fallen from, walking toward them. He didn't feel the burning of fear that he usually did, he instead felt the boiling of something new; something he rarely felt and had suppressed very well in his recent years. Anger, hatred, he hungered for revenge. The visions of all the bullying over the years swarmed him, buried his empathy, compassion, he felt himself walk up onto the group, fire in his eyes and heart which spread to the rest of his body.

"Hey wimp," the wolf sneered, oh how he sneered. Those white teeth cocksure like they always were. In one swoop of his paw the kangaroo whipped that expression off of the face. His bully was on the floor, but he didn't stop; he couldn't stop. His paw met him again and again with increased strength. He began to enjoy it, to return the suffering that had been place on him. Oh how his screaming became musical to him. He continued and continued, and as he did a little voice in him told him to stop. At first that voice was ignored as all he could see was that smug sniggering face and he kept his attack on the now helpless wolf.

His voice within resounded again to stop, a little louder. The fires of anger started to taper as Garoo's vision returned to him and he fought off the blindness of rage. He saw the results of his work, the wolf he had hated was now a bloody mess, beaten and bruised, unstirring.

"No..." the kangaroo said, both in his vision and in his body, causing the snake who had planted the dark thoughts to tilt his head in wonderment.

"No!" Garoo shouted and yanked his paw from Shadis's to the snake's astonishment. The kangaroo stumbled back as he struggled to expunge the darkness that was implanted there, the need to revenge, this was not him.

"Impossible..." the pale snake, "I'm Shadis, the Deity of Darkness... you're just some lowly creature, do you really think you'll be able to break from my power?!"

Garoo did not respond as he continued to struggle and stepped back, unaware of his position. He bumped into the obsidian snake statue. From the statue an item fell to the floor which seemed to snap the roo out of his inner struggle. He looked down to the object which seemed to be some form of a hilt with strange carvings on it.

"No! Impossible!" The pale snake went to move quickly to stop the kangaroo from touching the fallen item, but he was too slow.

Another aura rose from the obsidian hilt and cut through the dark one that was working its way up the kangaroo's arm. It rushed him like a tsunami, all that bitterness, anger and hatred was washed away.

A cross-wind stopped the pale snake in his tracks, a claw raised to his face as a bright light aura started to replace the darker one he tried to implant. Shadis peered past his claw to the statue of the darker snake and he leered at it. "So this is your champion, huh brother? The one that'll bring the light? Well Luminis, you should know that, because you intervened, there will now be blood. There will be war, and all because you got involved..." he muttered as he looked back down to the kangaroo who now was physically healing as he was filled with the black snake's power of life and light.

Knowing that his cause was lost, the pale snake of darkness decided to make his egress. He used his power to transform into a raven, just as pale as his original form, and flew out of the hole and out into the world, abandoning the kangaroo to his kinder brother.

Garoo fell to his knees as he gripped the slab in his paw, he could see the wounds on his arm healing up quickly as this new power flowed through him. He saw the darkness of the room vanish away, the brightness of light flooding over him. The slab seemed to transform into a black snake. At first he was going to whip his paw away, but there was a sense of comfort in the creature. It did not act in a threatening manner as it slithered up his arm.

Then as it got up to his arm it bit him, but it was not a bite of aggression, he felt a rush throughout his body, almost paralyzing, however, there was no fear. He could see that this was his power, the long lost power of life and light, not through words but through action. The power healed his wounds from his fall, but there was so much more with this gift.

The kangaroo suddenly felt his heart sink as he saw a vision. He saw the shrine of Aquatis, Fangstro was there and so was Kareen. The wolf was strangling the otter, the otter was fading fast. She was on death's door. By the time he got out of this hole and back to the temple it'd be too late.

To see that future, his childhood friend dead on the floor of the water shrine, caused great sorrow. Garoo's fists clenched, he felt upset and he cried out. His tear fell into his paws, he felt the water rush over them, feeling powerful with this new gift but helpless to save his friend.

Then the tears started to fall through his paws, causing the kangaroo to give a bit of pause. He then felt instinct take over; though he didn't know how to use this power voluntarily, because of the catalyst of the vision it was happening of its own accord. Garoo was transforming from a physical form into one made of pure light. Time slowed to a standstill and he could see all the light streams around him, but also the walls of darkness.

His light form could move through the streams where light touched, but was hindered by dark, he could travel with the light, at its speed. He flowed out of the hole through the light streaming down it and up the cliff to the bridge. He needed to do all he could to save Kareen.

The dark-furred wolf squeezed his paws around the throat of the otter a bit harder. Closing his eyes, a bit of him wondered why he was doing this, but his mind went back to the two nights before at the dinner when she punched him in the nose. The burning of vengeance in his heart pushed his paws tighter around her throat. Her body started to go limp, she was losing consciousness and in her visions she felt the water fill her lungs, feeling herself let go to her fate of drowning.

It was at this point something caught the corner of Fangstro's eye, a brightness that seemed to arrive through the blue hues of the shrine's lighting. At first it was but a light glow, but then it grew to the point the wolf could no longer ignore it. His muzzle turned toward it, the strange glow was changing shape to the point where he could recognize it.

Instantly he went cold beneath his dark fur. His paws released his victim, causing her to immediately gasp for breath. Fangstro stepped back, his whole body trembling. "I—Impossible, you're dead." He truly felt he was seeing a ghost.

The light form started to materialize back into a physical manifestation. Garoo was silent as he now stood in the shrine of Aquatis, slowly moving toward the form of the otter, still lost in her vision, weak and short of breath. The kangaroo moved up to the platform she was on and placed a paw on her shoulder. She roused from her meditative state. "G-Garoo?" she asked in disbelief.

"Yes, it's me…"

Though the question of what he was doing there ran through her mind, she reached forward and gave him a hug. He returned it to her as he closed his eyes, "You're okay now."

But then Kareen realized something and released herself from her embrace wiping away the tears in her eyes. "Y-You shouldn't be here! You could be punished being here while I'm conversing with Aquatis."

Garoo looked down, "I know this." He put a paw to her neck, indicating her bruise and bringing the attempted strangulation to her notice, looking over to the wolf who had backed into a corner. "But I had to stop him from hurting you."

"Him?" the otter looked over to where Garoo was looking to see Fangstro. "Him! You! What did you do? Were you trying to kill me?" there was a bit of a rumble as she felt an energy deep within explode forth. A jet stream of water rushed forth from her paw and slammed the wolf into the wall. Against the sound of the stream one could barely hear the breaking of the shoulder of the interloper against the stone wall, causing the canine to let out a yelp.

A paw pulled the otter's shoulder to try and quell the storm of her newly-found power. "Stop. Please," the roo attempted to calm her and stop the attack on the wolf.

Kareen's attack tapered off as she lost energy and fell onto her knees, panting as her rage quelled. The soaked and injured wolf held his shoulder, still confused as to what was going on. He was shivering a bit, both from the physical coolness caused by having dampened fur and the fact that he was seeing a kangaroo who should be dead.

There was a slam of a door which caused the three to turn their heads to the previously-sealed entryway, a few monks of the temple barged in and made their way up to the meditation platform, an Elder and grey-muzzled wolf looked upon the scene before them and were not pleased.

"What in the Powers' names is going on in here? Only one is allowed in the chamber of elements during the transition! Two of you are transgressing! Who was the last one to be called into Aquatis's chamber?"

The monk who was calling out names from the drawn cards was among them, "Kareen."

"Kareen step forward," the Elder barked.

With a look of concern back to Garoo, the otter stepped forward when her name called, she was respectful and remained silent for the moment. As she stepped forward, the other temple monks ran past to the other two creatures who were not supposed to be there and grabbed them. Fangstro was lifted up harshly despite his injury, making him whimper in pain.

The grey-robed wolf glared to the two. "You two have committed a blasphemy to our temple and to the powers, your punishment will be swift and severe."

Kareen suddenly jolted to the robed one. "No! Please don't harm Garoo, he was just protecting me from Fangstro."

The Elder shook himself free. "Miss, it is highly irregular to lay one's paw on the cloth of a monk, unless you wish to suffer the same fate as these two, you'd best not transgress again."

Garoo and Fangstro were now standing side by side being held still by the monks who had surprising strength, but the earth mages had also bound the trespassers' wrists behind their back with some vines they had summoned.

"You two shall stand before the Sages in an emergency meeting, they will decide your punishment," he said as they were escorted out of the chamber. Kareen went to go to Garoo, to pull him away but he was moved too quickly and her paw only barely grazed him as they passed by. She was speechless, but she trembled as she feared for her friend's future.

"You are to go, too; you are a witness," the old wolf informed as he put a paw on her shoulder, knowing she was having a hard time of this, and escorted her from the room. As they left and the shrine of the giant sea turtle now stood alone again, the door closed with an echoing clang.

The four Sages and Lady Wollnutt went down the spiral stone stairwell, leaving the privacy of their chamber. A temple helper had summoned them to the gathering room, where guests typically spoke with the Sages. This wasn't a meeting of pleasantries, unfortunately; it was said that two creatures had committed a punishable offence and had caused a hindrance to the proceedings of the Transition.

"Not even your first day and you're already going to have the honor of kicking a creature square in the behind," the falcon Wind Sage quipped. "This job certainly has its perks."

The Fire Sage obviously wasn't a fan of such things. "Oh we haven't even heard their story yet, you always have an ax to grind."

"Better for one's ax to be ground, lest it be your head that rolls around," Sagacid retorted before adding the stinger. "Take that as companionship advice."

She ignored the intent of saying that she was acting too weak with her rebellious mate and turned it around. "Really? I didn't know you were into dismemberment, well then I guess I won't give you that pleasure, despite the urge for me to do so."

The Water Sage leaned to Bomeran as they had arrived to the gathering room and muttered. "With how they act you'd think they were life companions…"

Lady Wollnutt stopped outside the door and looked over to Bomeran. She was now in a plain grey dress, a simpler wardrobe indicating her now lower stature. The deer now wore his green robe, which he made sure not to trip over with every careful step. "I leave you now to make your first decision as a Sage, good luck, and lead wisely." She gave a hug to her friend as she turned around to head out of the temple and go to her awaiting children.

With a deep breath, the buck followed the other creatures into the room. He was not expecting to recognize the faces of the alleged troublemakers inside, however. "Garoo?" he called out to himself as if to convince his ears to what his eyes were seeing. The other Sages sat down at an elevated bench with four chairs. Bomeran joined them in sitting down seeing that indeed his son was one of the three youths before him. The other two were also creatures he recognized: Kareen and Fangstro.

He glared a bit at all three of them, but decided to hold his tongue, he would rather not cause a scene and would like to see how the other Sages handled the situation before adding his own, biased opinions.

As the senior member, Sagacid started the conversation. "It is of my greatest regret to inform you three that you have been brought before today because a great transgression has been committed upon the temple. Multiple people were found in the shrine of Aquatis during the process of Transition. This is unacceptable and the punishment will be severe. I wish to begin by getting your names so that we may be able to address each other. Of course, when addressing us you will use the traditional Sir or Lady. It's a bit insulting that I should have to remind you of such but knowing how you handle yourselves in our temple, I can't leave any stone unturned."

The three introduced themselves in turn, each a bit intimidated by the prospect of having the wrath of the Sages. The otter Kareen started by introducing herself, her eyes glanced over to her kangaroo friend in worry. Garoo stated his name second and kept his eyes over to look at his father who looked back toward him. Though his father was expressionless, the roo felt ashamed to be there, and his dad's presence made it all the worse. Lastly, Fangstro bitterly gave his name, grappling with his damaged shoulder that was distracting him from the weight of this trial. He certainly didn't want to harm his own chances at being chief, at least he had condolence that Garoo wouldn't be Elder, either.

The Water Sage was particularly irritated, being it was his shrine that was trespassed. "I was informed that Kareen was the only one authorized to be in there. I must ask if you had anything to do with this, young miss."

"Of course not Sir, I just meditated as is proper," she replied. "I had a vision of being submerged in water. When I came to, Garoo and Fangstro were both there, I do not know how they entered."

"Congratulations on your successful Transition to water, Kareen," Bomeran said, knowing it was always her biggest wish.

The Wind Sage returned the conversation to the current matter. "So that means both Garoo and Fangstro are the ones in transgression. I propose that both be banished."

Both the wolf and kangaroo sunk in their chairs a bit, banishment was nothing to take lightly. It was most certainly worse than being a forsaken. If one was banished they could not enter any township of their race, and would be treated as a hostile if they do so. Basically, they'd be treated as an enemy.

Knowing it was likely because his element's shrine that was infiltrated that Sir Anauran agreed with the bird's assessment, the Fire Sage dissented from that hasty action. "I believe we should at least hear out their side of the story, why they were in the shrine to begin with."

Sagacid shook his head and sighed. "What does it matter, it's essential that consultation with the powers happen on a one on one basis. Now, Kareen was able to succeed, but their interference might have done harm to the process. We've already had the issue with cargo being raided on the Arcane, I think this generation needs a swift reminder that they can't just go doing what they like."

Bomeran put his words in now that everyone else has had their say. "Let it be known that I know all three before us now, I was their Elder in the town of Emergant. I will do my best to make a sound decision based upon this bias, however I agree with the Lady. Let us hear each story and make a decision of punishment based upon it."

The eldest Sage looked over to the deer and gave it a think. "Hmm… well, I suppose last words are always entertaining in their own right." He turned to the antlered kangaroo, "Alright, we'll start with the mutt."

Bomeran glared over at the bird who uttered that word. "Address my son like that again, sir, and I'll assure you it will not rest well in your favor in future negotiations."

All three looked over the Bomeran with a mix of shock and dumbfounded expression. "Oh really?" Sagacid shook his head. "Alright then, my apologies, Garoo, go ahead. Be brief though, there are other things I want to get to today."

"I woke up late this morning and was in a hurry to get to the temple, I saw Fangstro climbing the outer walls so I did my best to follow him. He's been a troublemaker in our community so I knew he was up to no good. I followed him into Aquatis's chamber through this back route and kept an eye on him. I saw Kareen meditating and Fangstro began choking her. I came forward to put an end to that. Not too far after, the monks entered the chamber and here we are."

The Sages were taking down notes of the story as it was being told. Garoo didn't want to tell the whole story; something from within himself told him that divulging what had happened would sound too much like a tall tale. I mean, a hidden shrine and changing into light? Who would believe that?

The Wind Sage turned to Fangstro. "Now it's your turn."

"Like you would follow me without ratting me out to someone," Fangstro started by attacking the accusation. "I found myself awoken being dragged by Garoo here into the shrine, clearly he wanted to get me banished. When I awoke I started to fight back, which is how my shoulder was injured."

Kareen sighed, "Oh please! It was I who injured you, and you keep lying like that I'll do it again!"

Sir Sagacid shook his head. "A quaint waste of my time but it still doesn't change the fact that neither the wolf nor the kangaroo was permitted to be there. I still say both should be banished, as Fangstro had noted, Garoo could have called on the monks to handle the intrusion."

"Agreed," the Water Sage placed his vote with the Wind Sage.

The Fire Sage grinned. "Oh, so quick to judge, I'm calling a tangent punishment. Fangstro shall be banished, Garoo shall be unable to participate in the Transition."

Bomeran frowned. "Of course, you know my bias here, and I know my son wouldn't harm anyone, no less endanger Kareen from her consultation with Aquatis. I do think Fangstro should be banished, but I feel my son should not be punished in any way."

Fangstro growled. "This is bull! You have no proof that I would willingly break into the shrine, and you're just going to take it on the word of Garoo that I went in there to harm Kareen. What's my motive for that? You have none, this is just rigged in his favor because Garoo's father is amongst you."

The Sir of water shook his head and looked agitated at such an accusation. "I assure you young one, this is our own decision."

"But he does have a point, we don't really have a motive, so we should not show preferential treatment and banish them both," the Wind Sage countered.

Fangstro really didn't want to be banished, but he knew now he had no chance, he just wanted to assure that Garoo went down with him. "If we must both be banished then so be it, I'd rather there be justice done for both of us, for we had committed the same crime."

Sagacid turned to the other Sages. "I happen to agree, I know Sir Bomeran would never agree but what about you Lady Pardinia? Are you convinced to banish Garoo? That would make it three to one."

"Oh I did have something to add, but I assure you it's not I who will change my position today." With a clearing of her throat, Lady Pardinia sat up in her chair and leaned over on her feline paws staring down the wolf across the way. "Now Fangstro, have you been completely honest with us? If you haven't, I'll give you a chance to redeem yourself."

Fangstro growled. "Of course! Why am I the only one being accused of lying here? What Garoo did was just as wrong, and he could just as well be lying for all you know."

With those words, the lynx looked toward the door where a monk stood watch. She gave a nod to them, causing them to leave the room. "We both know that you aren't being truthful, Fangstro. Do you happen to know anything about what happened to the cargo aboard the Arcane?"

The wolf hopped up a bit in his seat, his ears folding back. "N-no. Why would I know anything about that? This doesn't have anything to do with the shrine."

"I'm not amused by your constant lying, Fangstro. This behavior has solidified my motion to banish you, however it has also made me wish to show Garoo leniency. If I were in the kangaroo's position, knowing the type of individual you are, I may not have wanted to chance leaving you from my sight." The Lady frowned.

The wolf a slammed his good paw on the table as he got agitated. "And where's your proof I'm lying? You seem so sure! You have no—"

If it were possible to see, the others would have seen the dark canine grow pale in complexion because the monk that had left had returned with another. There was a long pause until the wolf sunk back down into his chair as his heart followed suit.

The Lady explained the new arrival. "I'm sure you have met Sharlean, have you not Fangstro?"

There was no response from the wolf as he looked over to his sister. A look of pain filled her eyes as she returned her brother's stare, she saw the anger in him. She wished she had acted sooner, but she had acted, and now there was no turning back.

Pardinia was more than happy to explain the hard work she did to procure the witness. How when the dinner was banned and her people were unhappy that she took it upon herself to look into who could have possibly broken into the cargo. After a few dead ends she ended up running across a lone wolf. That was how she met Sharlean, and she told her everything, including the plot to make sure that neither Kareen nor Garoo would become Elder of Emergant.

"You see, unlike some Sages, I'm not afraid to get my paws dirty and investigate problems," the Fire Sage finished her monologue triumphantly.

"Is what all she said true, youngling?" Sagacid asked

The female gave a nod. "It's true, I would have reported it sooner, but he's my brother; I hesitated."

"Still Garoo should have told the monks instead of going in himself," the Water Sage noted, "he should still be punished in some degree, I move that he be not allowed to participate in the Transition as the Fire Sage first suggested."

"I third the motion," Sagacid shook his head. "I rarely say this, but good work, Lady."

They all looked to Bomeran, who had hardly spoken during this whole ordeal. He simply looked across to his son. He really wanted him to be blessed. He didn't want to be the one to seal his fate as a second class citizen. He remembered the pain his lost love and he, as a result, dealt with being in that position. However, the look Garoo gave was not of longing to be unpunished, but one of reassurance. That he knew what his father had to do, and that he accepted this as his fate. What a brave child he had raised.

"I apologize son, but I fourth the motion," he said with a heavy heart.

The Water Sage blinked… "We're in agreement? That's the first time we've been able to come to a decision without using Lament in a long while."

"You're welcome," quipped the Lady of Fire.

The fires in the sky spread its reddish hue across the stratosphere once again. The Day of Transition was coming to a close and most creatures had united with their element, along with an unfortunate few who hadn't. Garoo had made his way outside to get some fresh air, and to satisfy his curiosity. He had scooched himself to the edge of the bridge before the temple that stretched over the chasm. He sat and peered over the ledge as best as he could to the lands below, trying to find the room he had fallen into. How far could he have actually fallen? Unbeknownst to the kangaroo, his friend Kareen had arrived and saw what he was doing. She felt her heart sink with dread as she saw him looking down the cliffside as he sat at the bridge's edge. Without a word she ran up to him from behind grabbed him and pulled him back from the ledge, scaring him as he was tackled.

"Don't you dare even think about it! It's not worth it you hear!" the otter shouted at the roo she had pinned to the stone bridgeway.

Still a bit confused at the situation, Garoo looked up at her. "What are you talking about?"

She gave him a punch to the shoulder. "Don't play stupid! I know you're now forsaken but that is no reason to kill yourself!"

Garoo blinked, and then gave a laugh. "I was actually just getting some air; I wasn't going to take my own life. Our culture may consider me forsaken, but the Powers and I know that I am anything but."

This didn't make Kareen happy as she gave him another punch to the shoulder. "It's not funny, I was worried you were going to jump!" She frowned as she got off of him and used a paw to help him up.

The roo took the assistance and stood up, going back to the edge and looking down, he then saw what he was looking for. Not too far below the temple, about a score of feet there was a hole in what appeared to be a piece of the temple basement sticking out the cliff side. He waves over Kareen and points to the opening. "You see, I already fell down this cliff once before, and I have no wish to do it again."

Kareen looked closely, "That fall—that's a good several body lengths. How could you have not have been gravely injured?"

With a nod the kangaroo moved forward and sat at the bridge edge again, inviting his friend to sit beside him as he told her what had happened during the day. How Fangstro had caused him to fall, how he had found an old abandoned shrine. The strange entity who awakened a sickening darkness in his heart, and the other force which caused the being to flee. He was able to heal himself with that power. He was able to get to her when she was in peril. The otter believed this story, as she recalled seeing this lightly aura around him when she saw him in the shrine.

"I don't understand this power, if there is an element to it, but it certainly felt powerful when it was unlocked. Not so much now, though I feel it lingering still," he said.

"This normally happens when a transition occurs, like me with that water stream, excess energy from the initial infusion," Kareen explained. She then stood up. "We should tell the Sages! I mean, you're not forsaken and this is a new power! We have to tell someone!"

Garoo jumped up with a shake of his head, putting a paw on her shoulder. "No, no, no. I don't know what the rules are for going into that shrine. I could have done something punishable by entering that place. It was obviously sealed off from the looks of it. I don't think the temple would be happy of me breaking into another shrine."

The otter saw he had a point. "I see. But are you really okay with being considered forsaken?"

"I know what I am, even if others do not," he said, as more folks began to move along the bridge, until one stopped to greet the pair.

"Um… hey guys," came the voice of an old enemy, Sharlean, as she approached them.

Kareen didn't really respond, a little upset that the wolf didn't turn her brother in sooner, but Garoo gave her a smile. "Hey there. Thank you for doing what you did, it couldn't have been easy."

She looked down, "I truly am sorry for that."

"So I heard you obtained the element of fire, congratulations."

The emotionally distraught wolf gave a bit of a smile. "Yeah, like my father before me, I suppose now I don't know quite what to do now that this is all over. I mean, I'll be trained just as anyone else I suppose, but my destiny isn't all that clear. I spent so long just following my brother. My mother always treated him as our family's heir. I don't think she ever really knew his true nature. She'll find out now for certain."

In speaking of Fangstro, the dark wolf could be seen be seen exiting the temple, with two monk escorts. Garoo was the first to see him and go silent. Eventually the other two followed his glance. The dark wolf could see their eyes, peering at him and staring. He felt an anger bubble up at them. It was all their fault and now they come to stare at the show they created. How dare they!

In a swift motion, the wolf picked a dagger out of an escort's belt and charged at them. In his blind rage, he did not care where his dagger fell, but Kareen happened to be the closest target. He let out a howling battle cry as he charged.

Garoo felt something click within him. While the other two stood frozen, he quickly pushed Kareen to the side. As the dark wolf raised his dagger to swing it down, the kangaroo balanced on his tail and pushed forward with both feet. The devastating kick landed square in the canine's stomach instantly causing him to drop the knife, which flung off the side of the bridge into the waters below.

The mages responded quickly to the scene now that everyone had stopped to notice, a land monk used vines to bind the wolf's paws behind his back. "We thought you'd have enough dignity in you to not be thrown out in shackles! Clearly we were mistaken!"

The wolf glared at the three as he was hoisted back to his feet, now restrained.

"I really do hope that's the last we see of him," Sharlean said, paining to say that about her own brother, but he really had become a monster.

Kareen finished standing up, she walked over to Garoo, and wrapped her arms around him. "You not only saved my life there, but you also stood up to him! By the Powers, you finally stood up to him! Bomeran would be so proud," she smiled. She had a look in her eye, one that the kangaroo had seen on occasion, but never to this intensity. The otter started to draw her muzzle closer to his.

"Indeed I am, young lady!" the booming voice of the Land Sage cut through the moment and caused the otter to suddenly jump back from her position, letting the roo go so he could stand before his father.

"I apologize that I had to come to that decision, son. You did violate one of our traditions to a high degree. I did all I could with what I have, and I have Lady Pardinia and Sharlean to thank for that." He gave her a nod of gratitude. "You are like your mother in so many ways, but from what I just witnessed, you do have the ability to defend when the time calls for it. You did so by pursuing Fangstro into the chamber and with what I witnessed just now. My fears about you not taking any action in the face of wrongs were not justified."

Kareen looked to the Sage and asked him the question. "So is he going to be the Elder of Emergant or am I?"

"As much as I'd love to pass the title to my son, he's a forsaken. They cannot hold leadership positions by laws that are even above us mortal Sages. It therefore must fall to you, Kareen."

The otter really wanted to tell him about the power Garoo had, that he really wasn't forsaken. She wanted him to lead instead of her. She glanced over to him with a bit of a plea, but the kangaroo shook his head in return. Kareen sighed and resigned to her friend's wish and remained silent.

With the pause, Bomeran decided to end the conversation so they could absorb the day's events. "Anyway there'll be more time for this later, let us go celebrate tonight. Now that we know who messed with the cargo and that is taken care of, the village has allowed us the opportunity to at least have the feast that comes at Transition's end."

Garoo felt the earthquake in his stomach and the water fall from his mouth in hunger. In all the excitement he had forgotten how little he had gotten to eat during the past couple of days. Finally he was at enough peace to get some long-overdue nourishment.

# Chapter 5
# Looming of Shadow

A high, shrill sound echoed across the swamp, snapping Fangstro out of his uneasy slumber. His fur was matted with twigs and mud from the lands he had stumbled across looking for signs of civilization. He found a few towns, but word spread surprisingly fast. What he was hoping to find was another race's settlement, though on this continent they were rare. He was still very worried about how he would be received.

The Farawlz were rather uncivilized and brutal even to their own, so Fangstro had no doubt an outsider would be treated worse. He didn't know much about the Domistechs; their cities were now mostly ghost towns. He'd only heard of a few that had been spotted about the surface. They were known to either run or join local towns as forsaken. Maybe if he was lucky he could find some that were hiding and would be willing to take him in.

He doubted anyone would have settled in this swamp, but he had no choice; he was driven into it at the last town. His paw moved up to his muzzle, there was no longer the feeling of blood trickling down, but he felt a scab there.

It was a horrible nightmare, one that had lasted many days, or at least it seemed like days: scraping up what he could find for food and following the waterways to get a drink whenever he needed. Here though, nothing was drinkable and seemed to be just a nasty soup.

Fangstro cried out as he found his body tumble forward with a sudden change in the misty swamp floor. His entire body was suddenly consumed in murky and viscous fluid. He kicked and thrashed about as he tried to get his head above water. His paws grasped at the land when they suddenly felt something completely unexpected: a paw gripped his own and hoisted him out of the sludge.

As he was back on solid ground, the paw let him go. The saved wolf coughed and gagged, he felt himself growing agitated at this life he was suffering through. He was angry at the fates, but mostly at the ones involved in the decision that forced him to live out this life. After his lungs were clear he let out a roaring howl, just trying to get all that anger out.

He opened his eyes with panting breath to see the form that had helped him out of the muck. A pale naga stood before him, a bit of a smile on its face. The wolf's tail and ears sank down low as he looked at the large snake, his eyes looking about for a weapon to defend himself.

"Oh dear, I didn't mean to frighten you with my appearance. I just get so used to my natural form," the being apologized. A dark cloud surrounded him for a moment before it cleared to reveal a new form. The snake had become a wolf with similar features as Fangstro, however, instead of having a dark coat, its coat was just as white as when the being was in naga form. At this point

Fangstro was more confused, had he eaten something earlier that was causing him hallucinations?

A free stump was nearby and the strange pale creature sat upon it. "My name is Shadis, I am a deity of your race—"

"They're no longer my race," the wolf injected.

"Oh, no, they're your race. You were born of them, though they can reject you, I assure you the Powers make no mistakes. You may seem banished, you may seem forsaken, but you have something inside you. Something that they fear... it's why they threw you out."

The wolf gave a sigh as he shook his head. "Yet here I am without any magical ability or home to call my own, yet you say I'm something to be feared? I must be delusional, this swamp must be messing with my mind." He began to move away.

"I assure you you're not hallucinating, my dear child. I'm sure you have many more pressing questions on your mind. Like how your roo friend managed to survive that fall. Yes, I could sense that question runs deep within you."

The wolf's ears picked back up as he looked confused at the canine form before him. Even if this was an act of his imagination, he certainly had nothing better to do at this point, "I'm listening."

"You see, there are two deities that your legends no longer mention. At least, not to your common folk lore. Our shrines were sealed away for generations for fear of the prophecy of a Sage long before even your great war. I am Shadis and my brother is Luminis. I could read your memory, and saw you knock the roo off that bridge. He fell into our shrine, and when his blood hit the floor I had awakened. I thought I could take him for myself, but my scheming brother took him instead. That's how the one you know as Garoo recovered from his injuries. He was also able to travel through light streams to the shrine where you tried to take the life of the otter.

"Neither I nor my brother give our powers lightly. My brother doesn't feel many deserve power at all. Myself, I don't think there are many worthy of what I have to offer.

"However, that kangaroo, my brother must have seen something in and he stole him from me!"

The wolf rolled his eyes. "And why should I care? If you want that weakling so bad, then clearly you can't be too picky. Why don't you go take him back? Some deity you are…" he was sick of hearing of Garoo, the very thought of him stirred anger within his heart. As the bitterness stirred, the wolf turned his back to Shadis. He just wanted to head away from the reminder of the life stolen from him.

He didn't get too far as a form before him slid up from shadows of a looming cypress tree. The odd feat of traveling through the shadow gave the wolf pause as the pale form of the snake deity reformed, giving a bit of a boisterous laugh as he did. "Oh no, no, pup—you misunderstand: I don't want the roo any longer. However, he and my brother need to be dealt with. I sense in you an anger and desire for revenge. I'm offering you the opportunity."

The wolf brushed off the offer. "Oh? Well, they think he's an ungifted forsaken. He can enjoy it, and suffer through it… I hope he lives a long life just so he can experience the contempt for as long as possible." He once again started to move away.

Shadis's smirk went unseen as he decided to try for an angle he knew would catch the wolf's attention: "So, the roo destroys your family's proud lineage and you're just going to let him go? What would your father think?"

With a quick turn the wolf spat. "You don't talk about my father! You don't know what he'd think!"

With a hiss, the snake slunk his way back over toward the wolf. He could see he touched the nerve he was looking for and now he just needed to direct that energy.

"I know your father was a driven warrior who would stop at nothing to defeat the enemy. He didn't stop fighting until the war took him. Who would think that his whelp would run away when someone dishonoured his legacy? I guess if you don't want my help I'll just take my leave—continue your life of just running away."

The pale snake started to turn away himself, mostly for show, because he knew what would follow. The outcast wolf took pause, he remember the stories his mother would tell him about his father. He felt ashamed. He felt this being was right, he was acting a coward. If the kangaroo was as weak as he claimed why should he run from him? Why not make him pay for what he did to him? To his family's legacy? "Wait—"

With a pause, the snake waited for the wolf to continue. "Yes?~"

"You're right—I'm of better blood than to flee like a coward!" Fangstro took a confident step forward. He felt a soaring hope that he had not felt in days, a chance to get back at Garoo, for humiliating him and making him an outcast. Him and his family, he could make them pay.

The deity grinned. "Yes, I can sense your wish for vengeance." He reached his white paw forward like he did with Garoo in the shrine. "Just take my paw, and your destiny will be yours."

The Arcane had returned the new adults to their homes, blessed by the powers, and ready to start their new lives studying their elements. There were a variety of different ways to use their new gifts, and many opportunities. Some still had no clue what they were destined to do, while others' paths were crystal clear.

Kareen's first task was to meet with Bomeran at the chief's hut. There he would tell her what she needed to know for the job ahead of her. While she wasn't looking forward to the job, at least Emergant was a coastal town, she could still probably find some recreation in some fishing on the side. She looked to the meeting hall and gave a sigh as she entered the building, once again the deer was waiting and sitting on the central floor on his pillow. The otter sat across from him. She knew she should be focused on the current matter, but her guilt over Garoo's situation lingered.

As she sat, the old chief stood up. He had a wooden gnarled staff in his hoof. He placed it before the otter. Both stared at the symbol of the Elder of Emergant. "I certainly didn't expect to be passing this on so quickly, but I entrust this to you."

After a pause, she took hold of the item. The otter maintained her somber look as she looked down on it. "So what do I do now?"

Bomeran gave a laugh. "Fear not, a similar question went through me the first time I took the Emergant Staff as well. Before I bore you with advice, though, I do have to pass to you an important prophecy that only the Elders are allowed to know. It's probably not going to be of use, as it has yet to be. It, however, is a traditional tale that is passed down from leader to successor."

"Storytelling isn't my strong point, I was hoping to live my own story more than anything."

"You'll learn in time," Bomeran said before he began his tale.

The buck started to tell the story long lost from the minds of most of their race. That many generations prior to the Tri-Societal War there was another conflict that had been lost and forgotten under the shadow of the much more deadly war. There was a fifth shrine that held an untold power, one that many of their people had consulted during their transitions, but none took hold.

Represented by two snakes, the one of pale skin and the one of dark skin. It was said that maybe only once every several generations would be one able to confide their power. Many transitions came and went without a single blessing from it. The shrine with two deities looking over its center represented two elements as opposed to only one. One element, of life and light and the other of darkness and death. Many of the monks thought that it was too risky and that it should be locked away, however others stood by the tradition that demanded it stay open.

One day though, the deity of darkness, Shadis, forced a decision—a youth who went into the shrine came out a monster. At first the tainted one seemed normal, but after he went out into the temple halls, he picked up a decorative weapon and started to slaughter the youth awaiting to enter the shrines themselves. There was mass fleeing of the powerless as the monks did battle with this one darkened soul. It proved far too much for them to handle and many lost their lives. The Sages finally arrived on the scene and put an end to the tirade. The one who had been gifted was killed. It was then decided unanimously amongst the Sages that the shrine be sealed off.

However, during the night, after they had sealed the shrine, they received a vision that one day the power would be unsealed once again. They saw the light deity of Luminis choose a champion amongst them, but, as he did, in the shadow of this joyous event, Shadis also picked another to represent the darkness. They saw great conflict amongst their people.

The prophecy was vague as they always were. It was the job of each Elder to watch the youth amongst them for a sign that Luminis or Shadis has given their power, and to report this to the Sages.

As the story progressed, the look upon the otter's face became more filled with discomfort. This story, and the story Garoo had told her, and that aura she had seen. It all made sense, and fit the tale perfectly. She had a promise to her friend though, she bit her lip.

"Probably unlikely now that the shrine has been sealed. Even so, it's important that the Elders keep an eye out for any signs that this prophecy could come to light. You're to inform the Sages if there is an indication of such an event." As he finished up passing on his knowledge, Bomeran noted her unease. "Is there something bothering you, Kareen?"

The otter gave a sigh, she had promised Garoo she would not tell, but now as an Elder she had a duty to tell Bomeran. The otter struggled with the conflicting interests.

The buck moved to the side and put a hoof upon her shoulder. "It's a bit overwhelming, but if anyone can handle it you can. It should be easier in these more peaceful times, and I promise to do everything in my power to keep it that way."

Kareen looked to the floor. This was bigger than her and Garoo. If the prophecy was true, her holding back this information could do damage if the Sages were kept ignorant. She had to tell, and she had to do it now with someone who trusted her. "It's not that—I promised Garoo I wouldn't tell you—he was worried the Sages would punish him if they knew the truth. If someone did go into that shrine would they be banished?"

With a curious glance the buck replied. "I'm not sure what the punishment is, since it was sealed I don't think trespass would be taken lightly."

She gave another bite of her lip, but then gave a sigh and let it all out. She told him the story that Garoo had told her. The shrine he fell into, how he traveled almost instantly into the water shrine, how she saw that light aura about him during the confrontation with Fangstro.

Bomeran sat up, ears perking up as he looked to her a bit sternly. This was a bit too much for him to believe to be true. "I—I haven't known you to be the dishonest sort Kareen, this isn't something to joke about."

"I'm not lying! I told you, I'm no good at telling stories." Now that it was all out there she worried if Garoo would be punished. "What's going to happen with Garoo? Are you going to tell the other Sages? He didn't trespass the abandoned shrine on purpose. It was an accident!"

The deer stood up. Though it seemed unbelievable, he would go see it for himself. "First, I'm going to speak with him with you. If he is filled with Luminis's power I highly doubt we'd banish him or do any harm. The power he holds, none have been recorded to hold. It's highly mysterious, though it's rumored to be the opposite of Shadis's power, and if that's the case we have nothing to fear from him. In fact, if the other part of the prophecy is true, we'll need him to stand against the coming darkness."

As the buck went to the door he indicated to Kareen to follow, "I pray to The Powers that the darkness part of the prophecy is wrong, but in case it isn't, we haven't a moment to spare."

The abode that Sharlean and her brother had called home in Emergant was pretty spacious. Bomeran had made sure to accommodate his late friend's family well. In the center living space, a well-crafted stone fireplace took up a back wall. Above it, a unique weapon sat upon a mantle: a sword used by the wolf who was the Elder of Emergant during the Tri-Societal war. The blade was not a typical longsword. While one edge that was a sharp smooth blade, the other edge was ridged like that of a saw. This bladesaw, like most of the weapons of their race, could be used not only in combat, but also during times of peace to saw down trees for lumber.

The daughter of the warrior who once wielded that blade looked up at it. She wondered if she had done right by the father she had never met. Would he have done as she had?

She didn't have much time to worry about how her father would have taken this news, as she looked to deliver it to her surviving parent. Her eyes turned to the older wolf in the room, sitting in her chair before the fire. Sharlean wondered if she should tell her that her brother had died rather than to tell her what he had done. Whether it was now habit to protect her brother from trouble, or to avoid it herself, she didn't know. However, it was clear that her mother was already suspicious because she did not see Fangstro get off the boat.

She sat across from her mother as she told her the tale of what Fangstro had become in his hatred of Kareen and Garoo, of how he had little respect of the offerings being shipped. It took her all the courage she had to come to the story's conclusion, that her brother had been banished, that her mother's son would never return home to her again.

At first the mother felt disbelief in the story she was told. "How could this be true?" her body quivered as she spoke, trying to appear strong for her child, a role she had adapted as a single parent. However, when she saw the look of mourning in her daughter's eyes she could tell that her child was serious. As the silence settled, she started to doubt her disbelief. She went back to think of those times when her son might have shown signs of this nature. The stories she sometimes heard about her son causing trouble for the other young ones in town that she felt were exaggerated now seemed more prominent in her mind. As she continued to backtrack for clues she asked herself aloud, "How could I have been so blind? When—Where did I do wrong by him?"

"Don't blame yourself mother, he was the one who did what he did. You did your very best to raise us on your own. I am more responsible, as his sibling I could have stepped in sooner," her daughter said somberly as she looked down in shame, feeling some fault herself.

Sharlean felt her mother's paw rest on her shoulder. "Don't blame yourself child—I'm pleased that I did well by you. You hold the same flame as your father had, so I know his legacy will live on through you." She removed her paw as she began to move toward Fangstro's old room. Her strength holding back the sorrow was waning as the story echoed in the older wolf's skull. Deep down, though, she did feel she had let her love down by what had happened to their son. She didn't want her daughter to see her like this.

Her concerned daughter followed, "Are you going to be okay?"

The parent entered the abandoned room, turning to her daughter she gave her bit of a nod, holding her emotions back. "If you wouldn't mind, can I have a moment to myself?"

Respectful of her mother's wish, Sharlean was holding back tears of her own, relieved that her mother appeared she would be okay. Her mother really loved Fangstro, even spoiled him a bit at times. She figured the older wolf had experienced loss of those she loved before and perhaps that had hardened her a bit to such bad news. After all, those of her generation it was not an uncommon occurrence to lose loved ones.

"Alright Mom, call me if you need me. I'll be outside at the water hole to take a bath. It was a long trip." The younger wolf gave her mother a hug before she left her alone in Fangstro's room.

The afternoon light entered through the window as Fangstro's mother looked to her son's bed. She sat upon the mattress and placed a paw down on the pillow, tears falling from her muzzle onto the sheets. Her paws clasped around the pillow as she hugged it to her, though she knew he was alive out there somewhere, it didn't help console her.

"I never got to say goodbye," she choked aloud to herself. He might as well have been dead with such a sentence. For her, it was a fate worse than had he been killed, now she was in a perpetual state of worry. She wondered where he was and if he was safe.

Unbeknownst to the worrying mother, a silhouette stood by the door frame—a dark wolf who had returned to see his room one last time. As he stepped into the room, his mother heard his approach.

The mourning canine released the pillow, at first thinking her daughter had returned. "Sharlean I thought I told you to—"

There was a strong silence as the canine sat there, stunned. It couldn't be, but it was! Not thinking about the questions as to how he had gotten there, she jumped up and ran to her returned son and gave him a loving embrace. "Fangstro!"

Garoo looked upon the familiar docks on the bay, waiting for Kareen's return. Nearby, Urand was waiting for his sister as well, but decided he might as well practice with his elemental abilities while he was standing around. The bear had found a random weed and focused on it, trying to make it sprout further. Oddly, he was one of only a few from the town who was gifted with the element of land.

"I wonder how long the whole process takes," the kangaroo said as he leaned against the boating supply shed.

The bear's paws glowed a distinct green color as the weeds shifted, but they didn't grow. "Not too sure, I'm still trying to get over the fact that she'll be in charge of things around here." He gave a bit of a laugh. "Was bad enough when she didn't have actual authority."

"She'll do fine, I'm sure."

Urand stopped his focus as he turned to face his friend. He had heard about the fate that befell the roo, and he was worried how Garoo was taking it. "What about yourself, are you going to be fine?"

With a sigh Garoo stopped leaning back, grabbing a hold of his tail and pulling free a burdock that had gotten stuck there. "I don't know. I spent my whole life wondering what element I'd be gifted. I ended up with something I never even conceived."

"Being forsaken certainly can't be a joyful experience. However, I was your friend before the transition and what the fates decided will not change that. I'm sure that being the son of a Sage though, you won't be so bad off."

Garoo frowned. "That just makes me feel guilty. That because of who my father is I don't have to suffer as others like me must."

The bear shook his head and gave a hearty laugh. "Oh, and how is that any different than me being treated better than you just because I have some magical power? The world's full of these kind of things, don't feel guilty about who you are."

"I still feel a bit disappointed with myself, I wasn't able to let my father keep the Elder position in the family."

Urand shook his head and put his arm over the roo's shoulder, giving him a grin. "Oh, you'd like to think so. I figure your dad knows as well as I do that odds are giving it to Kareen will keep it in your family."

Garoo didn't know how to respond to that, as he leaned his ears back, a bit sheepish at how blunt his friend was about the relationship between him and the otter. There was another laugh heard, causing both of them to be startled. They soon turned to see Bomeran standing next to a flustered Kareen.

"Honestly that was not my intent, but I suppose it is a possibility." The deer gave a smile which only caused further embarrassment for Kareen and Garoo.

After that statement, there was a moment of awkward silence, one which the buck graciously broke as he looked to his son. "I need a moment with you, could you please follow me?" he asked before proceeding into the nearby shed. Kareen had a worried expression, which made Garoo suspicious. He didn't have time to question it though, as he followed his father into the building leaving the brother and sister alone out on the dock. Urand felt her staring him down for embarrassing her like that. He hoped they returned soon.

Once inside the shed the Land Sage looked among the gear in the room. He picked up a sharp-looking spear. "Son, I want to let you know that I'm proud of you. I've always known you to be the honest sort. So I must ask: why are you hiding your power from me?"

Garoo felt his heart leap in such a way that those of his species would be envious of the bound. His suspicions were confirmed. "She told you? She promised she wouldn't!"

"She told me because I told her about the shrine you saw first," Bomeran defended the otter. He then retold his son the story that he had shared with Kareen. He explained the relevance that the events his son went though had to the prophecy. "Only Elders are supposed to know about the lost elements of light and shadow; life and death. However, since you now seem to be in possession of this power, I think that it's important for you to know."

"So you're not mad? I'm not going to be punished?"

Bomeran shook his head. "I'm certainly not mad. More in shock, and mostly flattered that my son was chosen for such a responsibility. No other soul on this planet has the element you now possess. I must report it to the Sages, but fear not, for I am certain since it is the light you possess—and not the shadow—you shall be not punished or treated as a danger. However, while I trust you and Kareen, I must test this for myself."

Without warning the buck took the sharp spear and gashed the upper part of his arm. Garoo, shocked by this sudden action, rushed forward to grab the weapon and tried to pry it from his father's hooves. "Dad! What are you doing?"

His father let the weapon go as he had done sufficient damage causing his son to stumble back a bit. "I wanted to give you a test. The stories tell that those with the power of life should be able to heal other creatures. Focus your energy, son, and mend this wound. It's a minor injury and shouldn't require much energy."

The kangaroo placed the spear down into the rack it had been taken from. He then moved to examine the bleeding gash along his father's arm. "I'll try."

Garoo closed his eyes and focused his energy into his paw, pressing them against the wound. The warmth of his father's blood ran over his digits as he felt the energy flow from him to his father. A new warmth ran over his paws as the light gathered over them. Bomeran had to turn his eyes away from the intense brightness, even though he wanted to watch. He could feel the wound mend though, and felt the blood flow slow.

Soon thereafter the light began to fade away and the deer was able to unshield his eyes and look upon the area the wound once ached. He was astonished — not even a scar remained. It was as if there wasn't even any damage done to begin with.

Garoo stopped focusing and opened his own eyes, noting the awkward silence. He noticed the area of his father's arm had healed. Both stared to where the wound had been. The long emptiness and staring was starting to cause the roo concern; he wondered what his father was thinking.

"Father?" the marsupial broke the hiatus.

With that, the buck looked up and smiled to his son. Without a word he moved past him to the door and left the shed. As he returned to the dock area, he noticed that Kareen and Urand were still there, however the bear was on the ground and was dripping wet. Apparently his sister was not so quick to forgive him for his earlier 'embarrassing' joke.

Bomeran focused energy to his hooves, a green light gathered there and was bright enough to grab the otter and bear's attention. He shot the glow into the air and it soared up high into the air before it scattered into three different directions. The land's elemental flare would travel to the three other provinces to alert the other Sages. When they received that message they would make their way back to the Chamber of Sages in the Omnigic temple.

Just as the flare scattered, Garoo came out of the shed. His father turned to him. "Listen, Garoo, I need you to stay here while I return to the temple. Only the Sages and workers are allowed to go inside during the period between transitions. I'm sure after I inform them of this, they'll come to speak with you."

He then turned to the otter, "Kareen, keep the town safe in my absence. I shall return as fast as the land may carry me." Without further delay he made his way back to his home to gather supplies he would need for the journey ahead.

The mother embraced her son, taking in the feeling of his dark coat, a feeling she never thought she'd ever be able to feel again. She was so happy to see him there, her heart filled with joy. However, a scent on him smelled of the rough wilderness he had been through. There was a coldness to him now that she could feel. The story her daughter had told her returned to her memory and she moved back from her hug. Her joyous expression changed to one of sternness in an instant.

"You shouldn't be here Fangstro. Your sister told me all about what had happened. You were banished. You're putting our entire family in jeopardy by having returned here."

Realizing that his mother's demeanor had changed, the dark wolf frowned. "The only reason I was banished was because Bomeran was on the council. He has always been afraid of me. Of us! That our family would return to power as it should have been. Bomeran saw my father in me and didn't want to lose his power, so he cast me—"

"Enough!" the mother interrupted her child with surprising volume.

There was a moment of uneasy silence as she became teary-eyed. The evidence of how far gone her son was now before her. Bomeran was given that position by her late companion. It was not taken from him. Her son clearly was spiteful, and it pained her. The stories of what her child had done started to come back and anger took hold as she found her voice once again. "You are not your father! Your father was a wonderful Elder. He didn't care about the title or the power as you are rambling on about! He would have never dared eat of fruits that were not his, attempt to murder an innocent, or trespass our most holy of sanctuaries! You'll never be the creature he was!"

With her rage over, she turned her back to her son and moved to look out his bedroom window. "Leave. I will allow you to go peacefully this once. If you ever return, though, I cannot promise your safety and that I won't call upon others to forcefully cast you out of the village."

Fangstro looked upon the figure at the window in silence, shocked. He had never heard his mother take that descending tone with him ever before. He walked away in stunned silence but within a few steps an anger started to bubble, a dark aura starting to build around his paws. At about that time his eyes fell upon his father's blade as it sat upon the mantle. Something about the weapon called to him, and he answered it by picking it up. The darkness of his paw flowed over his father's heirloom.

The young wolf turned back to face his old room, moving back toward it with the weapon in paw. If his mother could not see his father's greatness within him, then he would show it to her.

Kareen moved along the path back to the Elder's hut briskly. After Bomeran had left, she didn't wait around to speak to Garoo. She had felt guilty having broken her promise to him, but the kangaroo had pursued. "Kareen! Wait up!"

Despite the call, she kept on moving and didn't look back, her friend gaining ground. Garoo hopped forward to gain even more speed realizing she wasn't going to halt. "Would you just wait? Slow down! I just want to—"

The otter suddenly stopped to turn around, her follower almost stumbling at the sudden change in pace. "Just want to what? Lecture me on how I broke my promise not to tell your father? Well I don't want to hear it! What was I supposed to do? Those stories he told me matched with what you told me! I had to tell him! I—"

The roo put a paw up to Kareen's rambling muzzle to silence her defensive words. He was calm as he tried to pass on that feeling to his friend. "Kareen, stop. I know all this. Dad told me. Don't beat yourself up. You did the right thing."

As there was a pause of silence it was clear that the situation had become less tense. Kareen took a deep breath as she reached up to remove Garoo's paw from her muzzle. "Did I?" she asked before thinking over what she wanted to tell him next. She wanted to tell him how much this revelation made her worry for him. That she was afraid that his being a light mage would mean he'd be taken away from the village... their village. At least when he was seen as forsaken, she knew that he would be close by and unbothered. Now that he was gifted, who knows what would be asked of him or where he would go? She was afraid he would be taken away from her.

It was now or never to let her feelings be known. With a sigh she took his paws in hers "Garoo, I—"

Before she could begin, there was a blood-curdling scream. "Did you hear that?" the roo asked as his ears shot up.

A call for help soon followed, it was definitely coming in the direction of Sharlean's residence. Without another word, Kareen let go of Garoo's paws and rushed toward the cries, the kangaroo following her.

Sharlean was outside wearing a very distraught expression. A few of the other villagers had gathered around trying to calm her down to figure out what was wrong. The otter made her way to the wolf as she was breathing heavily after her yelling.

"What is going on, Sharlean? Are you alright?" Kareen asked.

She looked up to the otter through tear-filled eyes as she pointed toward her home, paw trembling. "M-My mother—she's dead."

Kareen felt herself shocked by the words, while Sharlean's mother was older she was still in good health. The first thing that came to otter's mind was the concern that hearing the news about Fangstro was too much for the parent to take and she took her own life. For now, she kept her suspicions to herself as she wished to investigate the scene herself. "Can Garoo and I take a look?"

The wolf looked between the two before giving a somber nod, she escorted them inside at a slow pace. Not ready to see her mother in that state again, she lead them to the outside of Fangstro's room before she gestured them to enter.

When they entered the room they found the victim's body laying on the floor by her son's bed. A pool of her blood had gathered along the floor boards. Sharlean could be heard sobbing by the door as she had peeked in, but quickly regretted the decision. Forlorn, the kangaroo and otter looked to each other. Kareen took a deep breath as she moved forward toward the body. She knelt by it looking at the wounds. After a few moments she signaled for Garoo to come over and join her.

As soon as the kangaroo was in range to hear her, Kareen told her what she thought, keeping her voice down as not to disturb the mourning daughter in the other room. "I at first thought this might be a suicide, but I'm now leaning toward that she was killed. These wounds were clearly caused by a weapon, but there is no weapon in the room. Listen Garoo, I'm not sure if you have the ability, but can you try to use them to heal her? Her spirit may not have left her yet."

Something about the request didn't sit right with the kangaroo as he glanced back out to see Sharlean standing just outside the door, still in the mindset of keeping his abilities a secret. "I don't think that's a good idea, I mean how would we explain this to Sharlean?"

"Listen Garoo, everyone's probably going to know about your gift when all the Sages show up." The otter grabbed her friend's paw and pressed it to body on the floor. "Just do it."

With a sigh the kangaroo conceded as he closed his eyes to focus as he did with his father. Immediately he felt a wall stopping him, as there was no life to draw from in the creature he tried to heal. "She's dead, I cannot revi—"

The sentence was cut off as the healer felt a chill run up his paw and through his body. A darkness seemed to fester in the wound he held. He felt the unnatural force climb up into his own being and react with his own energies. Kareen and Sharlean seemed to fade from the roo's view while the room remained. The body on the floor felt a bit warmer, and a new form stood nearby, a blade in his paw with a serrated edge.

"Fangstro!" Garoo said with shock as he saw the weapon in the wolf's paw stained with the evidence of the deed he had just committed. The creature didn't react to the kangaroo's presence causing Garoo to feel that this must be some kind of vision. Judging from what he was seeing it was probably of the past.

The son stood over his mother. The expression on his face appeared empty. Garoo could see a darkness in him, it was strong, it reminded him of the white snake he had met in the shrine. The wolf knelt over his mother and looked upon his work. "This was so unnecessary, but I will not be mocked and cast out. It's too bad you could not see my greatness. All those who tried to hold me back will pay for their crimes."

As soon as those words were said the wolf stood up and his eyes fell upon a figure outside his bedroom window. The green robed buck had his bow and a satchel as he went out down the path out of the village heading north to the Omnigic temple. Fangstro grinned, as Garoo turned to him a fear took his heart.

The wolf started to move out of the room, blade still in paw. "And who better to start off than the creature who humiliated and banished me?" he asked himself as he moved out of the room.

Garoo went to move after the wolf to stop him but as soon as his paw left the corpse on the floor he snapped out of his vision. Kareen was plainly visible again as she had a hold of the kangaroo, Sharlean had also entered the room. The otter was shaking him, "Garoo? Come on, Garoo, snap out of it."

Sharlean was a bit agitated. "I don't know what's going on here, but you can kindly get out if you are not going to help find out what happened to my mother."

"I saw it, it was Fangstro… he took a bladesaw and attacked his mother! I saw him standing here!"

As soon as the kangaroo said 'bladesaw', the mourning daughter thought of her father's weapon and ran out of the room. "It's gone!" she called out before running back to the room. "My father's weapon is gone. How do you know it was my brother who took it?"

Before Kareen could explain to Sharlean what was happening, the kangaroo looked out the window seeing the path north from the village that his father had taken. Garoo got up and ran past the two females out the door. "Garoo? Where are you going?!" Kareen got up and chased after the kangaroo.

The buck Sage had made good time during the afternoon. He had spent many years in these woods and knew the most efficient way to travel through them on hoof. The sky's fire was making better time, however, and soon its light would fade from view, blanketing the world in darkness. His ear twitched as he heard the trickle of a nearby brook, causing his dry muzzle to remind him of how parched he was. His satchel of water had drained an hour ago and he needed to restock.

The orange glow of the late afternoon reflected off the flowing stream as Bomeran approached. He looked upon his own reflection as it wavered within the clear surface, looking at his most prominent battle scar: his asymmetric antlers. He closed his eyes and sighed, trying to put the event in which he obtained the anomaly out of his mind. He had hoped that his children wouldn't have to face such things he faced, see the kind of pain he'd seen, but, should the prophecy be true, this hope would not be realized. In fact, his sons might see darkness and nightmares beyond what even he had witnessed.

He opened his eyes again and sighed, thinking about these things was not important, and though traveling about in darkness could prove dangerous, he decided against setting up camp. If he continued at this pace, he'd be there by the late morning. The buck placed his satchel into the river and allowed the liquid to fill up the container before sealing it up. He managed to scoop up some water with his front hooves and splash himself before leaning down and drinking some straight from the source to cool off and hydrate before continuing his trek. These long journeys certainly weren't something he was used to doing so much in these times of peace. A part of him wondered how he ever managed such journeys so easily in his more youthful days.

The oranges of the sky that reflected from the water's surface were suddenly enveloped by a shadow. Was nightfall really already upon him?

As the buck looked up in wonderment of where the light had gone his eyes met with a glare of reflection upon a serrated blade in the paws of a dark silhouette that stood above him. Without a word the weapon bared down upon him. Old instincts took over as the stag's heart raced. He shifted his head to the side, aligning his antlers with the swinging blade to block it from its intended target. The sound of the clash could be heard throughout the forest as feral birds scattered from their nests. In taking this quick action Bomeran had prevented his head from being cleaved clean off.

The aggressor was not anticipating for the blow to be blocked. It now tried to get the blade free from the large rack. As the form struggled to free its weapon, Bomeran had a chance to look up and get a good view of his attacker.

The revelation was unpleasant, but at the same time was hardly shocking. While Bomeran had known that the wolf had never been the most good-natured of souls, he would have never had expected him to be as bold or foolish to attempt an assassination against a Sage. "Fangstro!" he snarled as his knee buckled a bit. He started to push back against the blade with his antlers. "Was banishment from our culture not enough? Do you wish to be banished from this existence as well?"

With a twist of his head, the buck jarred the blade from his opponent's paw, sending it to the ground several yards away. Now with the wolf disarmed, the buck was able to lunge forward at his attacker and grapple him around his waist, and pushed his way to the opposite side of the stream. As they reached the other shore the wolf fell over backwards and was now pinned by the older buck.

Fangstro could feel the sharp rocks pinch against his back as Bomeran had pushed his body down to keep him from getting away, all but his head was submerged in the streaming brook. He grinned up at the older creature without any fear despite his position. "Only the powers get to decide whose time it is to go to the depths. I am told it is your time old man, not mine."

"Then the messenger who told you this is a fraud and shall join you shortly!" the deer spat. He'd had enough of this. Though a creeping pain did fill his head with the realization that he would have to end the life of the wolf his long lost friend had called son, it was clear that any semblance this creature had to the noble family he was born had faded to nothingness by his multiple transgressions: first to his son, then to their culture, and now to a Sage. There was no other choice.

As the deer pushed the wolf's head under, he closed his eyes. He was a warrior; not a monster. He did not want to watch as the canine suffocated under the surface of the water. Feeling the form wriggling about under his hooves was hard enough to tolerate.

Suddenly the buck felt himself fall about a foot down into the stream. The surface splashed a bit as his own body submerged up to his shoulders. This unexpected turn of events caused him to open his eyes to notice that the wolf he held down was gone, replaced only by a shadow being cast upon him by foliage overlooking the bank.

There was a laughter that echoed throughout the area. Bomeran's eyes darted around to see where it was coming from but there was no one to be seen. "You dared to treat me as forsaken? It is all you who have been left behind! The Powers you worship are mere phantoms compared to the one who has found me." As Fangstro jeered, his form started to reappear, a liquid-like shadow form rose out from the shade. He had somehow merged with the shadows and now was coming out of them back into the physical plane.

"What sorcery is this?" the buck was motionless from his position in the river. He had been quite experienced in the magics of their race but, even with his knowledge of the elements, he had never seen anything like what he just witnessed. It was as he had feared. The prophecy was right. His son was the light and Fangstro the shadow.

Another concerning turn of events was that it seemed as if the wolf had a good handle on his abilities already. Most of their kind took a multitude of cycles of hard work to become comfortable with their gifts. It seemed as if the wolf was already casting some perplexing spells with relative ease.

As the buck stood up, his fur dripping with water, he felt the shock of the moment fade. Surely this was an unusual turn of events, but the Sage was confident that, despite the surprising ability, his opponent certainly couldn't stack up to one with his experience.

The wolf grinned as he reached down and picked up the blade he had lost earlier from the ground. "It's your ignorance that will be your downfall, you have no idea what you are getting yourself into."

"You're the one who has given themselves to an unknown power so unwittingly, and you call me ignorant?" Bomeran reached to his back and readied his bow.

As the string was drawn back and the weapon was aimed at him the wolf let out a laugh. "Do you really expect me to simply stand here and let you strike me?"

There was a flash of green aura around the buck as he looked to him somberly. "As a matter of fact..." he cut his own sentence off as he used his power. The ground trembled a bit before stone pillars shot up from the earth surrounding the wolf and cutting off all escape routes. The only opening was between the wolf and the archer. Without a moment to spare, the arrow released from the bow, and it soared to its target and hit the trapped wolf square in the chest.

A look of shock had filled the canine's eyes as he glanced down to the arrow which had impaled him before stumbling forward and falling to the ground. Seeing this, the archer let out a sigh as he put his bow away and stood up. He made his way up out of the river, moving to his downed target, not feeling enjoyment out of what he had done, but relief.

Despite clinging on to dear life, the wolf's mannerisms were oddly joyful. He seemed to laugh, despite the difficulty to do so having an arrow in his chest. His eyes seemed to look behind the deer as he stood over him.

"One truly enjoys death too much if they are laughing at their own," Bomeran said in response. This only caused the injured wolf to laugh harder. The Land Sage decided he had heard quite enough as he drew out a dagger to silence the wolf's mad cackling.

As he took out his knife the light started to fade from the world around him. The fire of the sky had gone beneath the horizon and night had returned to the land again. In an instant the form that was once laying before him on death's door had changed into a dark pliable mass and sunk into the shadows. The only thing that remained was the blood-stained arrow.

Bomeran paused a moment and he moved forward and picked up the arrow. As he did so that maniacal laughter of the wolf echoed within his head. The winds shifted about him and the fur on the back of the buck's neck stood up as he looked around. The darkness of night had seeped quickly into the crevices of the forest. If the wolf could travel amongst the shadow, he could be anywhere and could appear anywhere.

The buck saw him out of the corner of his eye, a few feet to his left. The Land Sage took his dagger, charged at the form, and with a lunge sank the blade into wolf's silhouette. It traveled through the shadow. It was a fake!

Before the stag could even bring his blade back from its attack he suddenly felt a sharp pain in his side. His hoof dropped his own dagger as he stumbled back and grabbed at the mortal wound in his torso. "H-how..." He fell back and his head grew lighter.

The wolf stood above the fallen Sage, at first he seemed to be shocked at his own power, but then he grinned as he brought up his blood stained weapon. "You have seen your last setting Bomeran, and soon the other Sages will share your fate." As the dark canine lifted the blade up to strike the final blow the stag closed his eyes, his thoughts went to his son and his prayers went to the Powers above that they would be there for his child—for he would not.

To Continue in
**Wind**

In the meantime...
Read other stories by
# T.S. McNally

"The Bouncer and the Didgeridoo of Awakenings"
found in
*Pulp! Two-Pawed Tales of Adventure*
edited by: Ianus J. Wolf

"The Curators"
found in
*The Furry Future*
edited by: Fred Patten

"Vermin's Vice"
found in
*Inhuman Acts: A Collection of Furry Noir*
edited by: Ocean Tigrox